PRIMAL CRIMES

AN ANNIE LONE STORY

CHARLES MALONE

DEDICATION

For Shannon, Jaden, and Madison.

ACKNOWLEDGMENTS

Thank you Barbara Parry. Your help with this project has been invaluable.

Kirby, thanks for loaning me your eyes for the cover. I couldn't have found a better pair of frightened eyes for the job.

CHAPTER 1

Hilda slowly regained consciousness and looked around the room. It took her eyes several minutes to focus. Her head pounded as if she had been hit in the head with a hammer. When she was finally able to see, she realized that she was in an unfamiliar place. She couldn't remember how she even got into this room, which immediately caused her heart to race. Where in the hell was she? More importantly, how had she gotten here? The room was filled with old furniture, broken workout equipment, and mountains of dust mixed with an overabundance of spider webs.

The room looked somewhat like an old storage closet except there was a modern whiteboard in the room with something written on it. She tried to make out what it was but she couldn't focus because her head was still foggy. Hilda tried to stand but she just fell over to one side knocking over a small end table. Her feet were bound with some type of metal restraints similar to old leg irons. Hilda's hands were also bound together with duct-tape; so much so that even her fingers were covered by the tape and felt numb because it was so tight. Though still feeling drowsy, Hilda knew at this moment that something was wrong. Her drowsiness began to give way to fear. She was scared. The most scared she'd ever been in her life. She didn't recognize a damned thing in this place. But her fear was fueled even more by the fact that she was restrained and couldn't move. Three questions started repeating themselves over and over again in her mind. Where am I? Who did this to me?

A door flew open at the top of some stairs and in walked a person wearing a ball cap that was pulled down tightly creating a shadow that obstructed most of the person's face but Hilda could see that the person had a square jaw. Who is this person she thought as adrenaline began coursing through her veins. Fear replaced the confusion she felt. What did this person want with her? Had she been accosted by some sick serial killer? One of those animals that likes to carve women up with knives. Torturing them until the women begged for mercy; making them promise to do anything to make the pain stop. Hilda's mind was consumed with some of the wildest thoughts imaginable.

"I see you're awake. Now the fun begins. I've been waiting for this for a long time. I've seen you running on Legion Way," said the ball-capped person who Hilda now knew was a man from his voice.

With the strong cold chill of fear growing inside her, Hilda winced at the thought that he had been watching her. Then all of a sudden it all came back to her. She had been running through downtown Olympia on Friday afternoon but that was the last thing she could remember no matter how hard she tried to recall what had happened. She had been kidnapped off the street in broad open daylight. Now she started to feel panic right in the middle of her chest. Had anyone seen her being taken in broad daylight? Had anyone even reported that she was missing? What had she done to deserve this? She couldn't understand why he would want to do this to her. Hilda tried to calm herself but her mind would only think of the worst. Her bones would be found weeks or months later strewn in the woods like some piece of garbage. She started to cry. She didn't want to die. She didn't want her life to come to an end at the hands of a mad man. A damned serial killer. Her mind didn't let her accept this as a fact. Her primal drive to survive kicked in with thoughts of what she could do to appease her abductor. She tried to reason with him.

"You don't have to do this. You don't have to kill me. I won't tell anybody if you just let me go," cried Hilda.

"Kill you? Why would I kill you?" chided the ball-capped man in a low tonal voice. "That would be a waste of a hot piece of ass if you ask me. I, personally, detest serial killers. What a loathsome bunch."

"You're going to rape me? Please don't."

"No, I'm going to make love to you."

"Please don't rape me."

"Why do you keep calling it rape? Its love-making. It's the natural order of things. Male and female together. Rape is such an ugly word. You shouldn't throw it around so casually," snorted the balled-capped man.

"But making love means that the other person is consensually participating in it. Right?"

"That's just what society tells you."

"I'm on my period now," added Hilda trying to do anything she can to stop what was about to happen.

"No you're not. I already checked."

"Oh God, don't do this to me. I've never done anything to you," begged Hilda now fully grasping the gravity of what was about to happen. This man who had kidnapped her was a crazy rapist intent on sexually violating her.

"I'm done talking about this."

"I'll scream if…"

"Go ahead. No one will hear you. And besides I really like it when *you* girls scream."

The ball-capped man took a knife out of a sheath lying on the table, which made her cringe at the sight of it. He slowly started cutting Hilda's shirt off, then her bra, followed by her shorts and underwear. With each motion, the touch of the blade's cold steel on her skin made her cry out loud. She considered trying to fight him but the presence of the knife made her reconsider. All that Hilda could think of was why had this man chosen her? What had she done to him? She hadn't done anything to him. Hell, she didn't even know this creepy animal. In her mind, she screamed why.

The ball-capped man removed the leg irons from her ankles before he unbuttoned his jeans and pushed them to the floor. As he stepped out of his jeans and finished getting undressed, Hilda stood and tried to run toward the open door at the top of the stairs. Before she made it to the stairs the ball-capped man grabbed her and threw her against a solid oak table in the middle of the room just in front of the whiteboard. As she lied against the table, the ball-capped man quickly inserted himself inside her from behind which caused her to jump with the surprise of what had just happened. As he began having his way with her, Hilda shouted "No." Her crying soon turned into a sob with the realization that she was helpless; she realized that what was taking place couldn't be undone.

"This feels good," grunted the ball-capped man. "I love you Hilda."

Hearing those words, Hilda struggled to get out of his grip and push away from the table to get him off of her but he was too heavy.

"Please don't do this," yelled Hilda.

"What's wrong? I love you."

"Get off me. You don't love me. Why would you attack me like this?" screamed Hilda.

"That's what I'm talking about. Keep saying that shit," replied the huffing and puffing ball-capped man as he began pumping in an out of her faster and faster savoring every last stroke with his head thrown back and his eyes closed. "This is only the beginning, baby."

Grasping how sick this bastard was for thinking he was in love with her made her sick to her stomach. So much so that she began to gag as if she were going to throw up but Hilda fought it back. Her biggest fear still remained. What still lingered in her mind was the question of what he was going to do to her after he finished. How was he going to kill her? She was sure that her parents would never hear from her again. Heck, they wouldn't even know what happened to her. Worst of all she wouldn't be able to tell them how much she loved them or make amends for any arguments they had had in the past. Her body would be tossed deep into one of national forests never to be seen again. Isn't that what they typically do? This scared her so much. She didn't want to die. Death terrified her.

"Are you going to kill me?"

"No. Why would I damage such a beautiful flower?" whispered the ball-capped man as he ran his fingers through Hilda's hair giving her an icy shiver right down her spine.

Hilda's cries grew even stronger with the realization that she was quite possibly going to survive this violent rape. The fear of being killed had so overtaken her earlier that now she felt somewhat comforted knowing that she was not going to die. With the realization that he was not going to kill her, Hilda needed to divorce her mind from what was taking place. She summoned the strength to do just that by looking around the room she was in for anything to distract herself from the violent thing being done to her. Hilda looked at the whiteboard in front of her and saw what looked like crazed propaganda. One phrase, among many, scrawled on the board read "DEREGULATE RAPE" while another read "REPEAL RCW 9A.44.040." Still another said "ALLOW MEN TO BE MEN." Her tear-filled eyes scanned the length of the board absorbing the psychotic statements written about women and sex crimes. The board was also filled with weird diagrams of female bodies with numbers on them, an array of photographs of women, and articles taped to the board about unsolved rapes in the south Puget Sound area.

The ball-capped man was in another world as he focused all his energy on thrusting in and out of Hilda. He felt like all of his dreams had come true. Here he was with a beautiful woman. A woman he had watched for many months. It felt so good to be inside her. When he felt his orgasm about to overtake him, he pulled her up off the table and began kissing her neck. She fought back the urge to vomit with each of his disgusting kisses. She wanted to push him away but she also didn't want him to hurt her so she let him continue. He breathed heavy into her ear with his final thrust at which point he grunted and unloaded volley after volley of his semen inside of her.

While he laid on her back after finishing, Hilda's eyes were filled with tears from what had just happened and she wanted to cry but she stifled her cries. She tried to remain in control. She didn't want to show him how much fear he had put in her because that would be giving him the last shred of her dignity and she wanted to maintain that much. She continued to absorb as much information about the place she was being held and about him as she could in an effort to be helpful to the police when the time came to speak up.

CHAPTER 2

Julia toddled out of her bedroom. The year and half-year old girl grabbed Annie's leg.

"Momma."

"Good Morning, baby girl," exclaimed a smiling Annie as she bent over to pick up the excited girl. "Let's get you some milk."

"Here you go, Annie," said Sibyl handing Annie a pre-made bottle of milk she had just taken from the refrigerator. "You want some bacon and eggs?"

"You don't have to make me anything, Sibyl."

"It's no problem. I'm already making bacon for myself," smiled Sibyl.

"Okay. I'll have some then. Thank you."

"No, thank you Annie for your friendship," added a grateful Sibyl who had nowhere to go when she was released from Mount Baker Corrections Center for Women (MBCCW) where she had suffered her own personal tragedy by being raped by the prison's Captain. Now, the forty year old Sibyl was no angel by any stretch of the imagination. Over five years earlier, Sibyl had a huge cocaine habit. She liked the excitement and energy she got from doing it but after being convicted for forgery for stealing her mother's checkbook and writing checks Sibyl was determined to clean her life up. While locked up in the county jail she was able to kick the physical addiction to cocaine, which was very painful. But then she had to do battle with the mental addiction that accompanied it and with the help of her mother and a drug treatment program in Canada, Sibyl became a productive member of society.

However, she met a man who presented himself as an entrepreneur with a variety of business interests but he turned out to be nothing more than a drug dealer. Sibyl learned about who he really was when she was arrested, charged, and convicted as the mastermind of a criminal drug organization based on *evidence* cooked up by her boyfriend to make it look like she was the ringleader in addition to his testimony against her at trial. That was how she wound up imprisoned at MBCCW with Annie.

But now that was all in her past. Annie had given Sibyl a new lease on life and she didn't plan on squandering that chance. She had already started filing applications at various area colleges in an attempt to finish her Bachelor's degree.

"You don't have to keep thanking me."

"I know but you've given me so much."

"Forget about it Sibyl. You would've done the same."

Deep down inside, Sibyl felt, for the first time in a long time, like she had a family; she was surrounded by people who loved her and she loved them. She didn't know any other way to show it.

While Sibyl stood over the stove with a happy smile on her face, Daryn exited her bedroom reading a copy of the *Olympia Herald*, the local newspaper.

"I can't believe how much evil goes on in this society today," Daryn said.

"What happened mom?" asked Annie.

"Oh, I'm just talking about that serial rapist running around

Olympia that they're talking about in the paper. Darn sickos everywhere you go."

"The police making any progress in the case?" Annie queried.

"Sure as hell doesn't seem like it. And let me correct you. Its cases," replied Daryn.

"How many cases?" Annie asked.

"Oh, I think four girls have been attacked by this nutcase," said Daryn looking at the newspaper to confirm it. "Yep, four!"

"It makes my blood boil just thinking about what these guys do to these women."

"Yes, I know. It's heart-wrenching to hear about that many women being brutalized. This used to be such a nice, quiet, and safe town until the yahoos started moving down from Lakewood and Tacoma."

"Mom, I don't think Lakewood and Tacoma have much to do with what this serial rapist has been doing. Anyhow, how do they know that he's a serial rapist?"

"This guy has been writing horrible things on the bodies of the victims."

"What kinds of things?"

"The paper doesn't have any of those details but it does say that he's a white male who wears a baseball cap that obscures his face during the commission of the crimes."

"Can we stop talking about this? It's giving me the willies," chimed in Sibyl as she placed bacon and eggs on each woman's plate.

"Sorry dear," replied Daryn taking a seat at the table. "I forgot."

"It's okay. It's just really hard; brings back bad memories."

They all felt a bit eerie talking about a serial rapist in their town as the room fell silent. But the women were soon distracted by the wonderful bacon and eggs Sibyl had made.

"Sibyl," cried Daryn with a mouthful of eggs, "what did you put in these eggs girl? Damn they are so good."

"It's a family secret," said Sibyl.

"Gosh, these are tasty," Annie added.

"My mom used to make these for us every Sunday morning when we were kids along with her famous pancakes," Sibyl replied.

"Where're the flapjacks," joked Daryn.

They all laughed. Then the women and Julia fell into silence for the next ten minutes as they devoured the yummy breakfast made by Sibyl. Sibyl felt proud that she could contribute something to the household that she had been invited into by her best friend Annie. As Annie finished up, the silence was broken as Julia began banging her empty milk bottle on the high chair next to Annie.

"Mom, I've got to see my officer today. Can you watch Julia for a little while so I can check-in? I don't like taking her to that DOC field office with all of those degenerates hanging around there," Annie said as she looked at Julia.

"Sure," smiled Daryn looking at Julia. "I don't mind watching pretty little Julie-Wulie."

"Thank you Mom you're a life saver. I'll see you guys later," said Annie as she kissed Julia on the cheek, grabbed her car keys, and scampered out the door. This would be the first time she checked-in with her Community Corrections Officer (CCO) in person for months. She had spent so much time traveling the United States, Canada, and Europe speaking to audiences at universities, women's groups, and civil rights organizations about her experiences at MBCCW where she had been sent to serve a sentence for having killed her violently abusive husband, Billy Lone. While there she encountered corruption and systemic sexual abuse of prison inmates. Although her incarceration was brief, it was life-changing. Unifying the abused women of MBCCW, Annie and her group shined a bright light on the crimes being committed by the prison staff. With the help of a raucous public petition campaign putting pressure on the governor, Annie received a conditional pardon that required her to be under the supervision of a CCO for one year. The CCO had given her a break on meetings by allowing her to leave the state and country for the speaking engagements as well as check-in by phone from her varied locations.

At first it was exciting to see all of these new places, meet all of the wonderful people who fought for the rights of women around the globe, and get paid to do it all. But after a while it grew tiring. With several dozen hotel rooms under her belt, she was happy to be home in her own bed, with her daughter, mother, and Sibyl. While she took Julia and Daryn to the speaking engagements in the U.S. and Canada, she traveled to Europe alone and, of course, she sorely missed that little ray of sunshine, Julia.

Hearing about a serial rapist unsettled her; this was supposed to be a carefree relaxing return home without any upcoming speaking engagements or other distractions. It was supposed to be purely family time. Her experience at MBCCW changed her. Whenever she heard about crimes against women she felt the need to do something. She felt an urge to look into these serial rapes but still being out on a conditional pardon, with about six months left until it became permanent, she thought she'd better just let the police do their job. Putting the key into the ignition, Annie thought surely the police will catch this guy sooner rather than later.

CHAPTER 3

The ball-capped man mopped the floor near the slowly awaking Hilda. She lay there staring at him. The anger she felt for him quickly resurfaced. Hilda was angry that he felt that he had a right to do this. With her anger flooding to the surface, she nearly burst.

"Why did you do this to me? I'm engaged to be married. I don't deserve this."

"You enjoyed it. The way you came for me was amazing," replied the ball-capped man.

"That wasn't me," sobbed Hilda.

"The hell it wasn't. I tasted that cream oozing out of your sweet pussy."

"You fucking disgust me you pig. Fuck you! Fuck you!" screamed Hilda.

"If I didn't have a schedule to keep, I'd give it to you again really good and make you cum again just to show you how much you really like it. We'll have this moment together forever."

"No matter what you say or do to me I know that it wasn't me. You can't control my mind," Hilda said.

Now she understood this sick fuck. He really wasn't going to kill her. Not this nut job. He wanted to make her live on knowing what he had done to her. This is what gave him joy. This is what made this broken fuck tick. She knew that he wanted her to suffer but she had other plans. She nearly had a complete mental picture of the room. She studied every last detail that she could. Absorbing the types of things that were in the room, the color of the walls, the fact that it was a basement of some type that she was in, and a variety of other things. She wanted to remember everything she could to help the police lock this animal up. She wanted to make sure she took away his freedom. This was her will power driving her. It was driving her to be strong. To not give in to his madness but doubts about the future of her crept into her mind.

What would her fiancé think of her now? Would he still want to marry her? Would she ever be able to love again once they found out that she had been raped? She knew that people treated rape victims differently when they learned what had happened to them. Maybe it would be best to just keep what happened to herself. But wouldn't it be wrong not to tell her future husband about what happened to her? Hilda's mind was consumed with questions and uncertainty. She completely forgot about being held captive and the fear of the situation.

He took out a syringe and, before she could protest, quickly injected Hilda with something. He removed the restraints securing her to the floor. In a manner of a few minutes, he removed Hilda's clothes and climbed atop of her and began having sex with her again.

She placed her head on her restrained arms to rest when a wave of exhaustion and the shot of whatever he had given her washed over her. She was exhausted. Before she could think another thought she fell into a deep sleep as the ball-capped man finished and withdrew from her limp body.

With a look of fear on his face, he quickly searched for a pulse. Finding that Hilda was still alive he relaxed. He picked her up and carried her over to a mattress on the floor in the far corner of the basement. After lying her carefully on the mattress, the ball-capped man brushed her hair from her face. He stared at her as if she was some prized possession.

"You are so beautiful, Hilda. I will cherish our time together," whispered the ball-capped man kissing her on the cheek. "Every single moment."

He moved her sleeping body over on the mattress making room for himself so that he could lie next to her. Stretching out on the mattress, he pulled her close and cuddled with her. This was one of the best moments of his life. But there was still one event that was his overall number one.

When he was just eight years old, he spent the summer with his cousin Lucas in Wyoming. He and Lucas had become blood brothers the previous summer and couldn't wait to get together again for another summer. They had planned to do more fishing, more secret hideout building, play more baseball and basketball, and other fun stuff than they had done all that prior summer.

When his mom dropped him off at his Aunt Sheila's house, he and Lucas were so excited that they both quickly greeted each other and ran off into the woods behind his aunt's house before he even said hello. His mom gave Aunt Sheila his luggage and spent about thirty minutes talking with her before hitting the road heading back to their house in Denver.

What a great summer it was, he and Lucas had a blast. One of their days was ruined, however, when Lucas' dad had to take him to a dental appointment for a cleaning. While Lucas was out, he simply watched television sitting on the couch waiting for his best friend to get back. Aunt Sheila came into the room and sat on the couch next to him.

"Are you having a good time here with us, Adam?" Aunt Sheila sweetly asked.

"For sure," he replied still staring at the show on the television.

"Would you like to spend every summer here with us?"

"Of course. This place is awesome."

"Good. Well, I want to let you know that you're welcome here every summer if you wish. But you have to be able to keep a secret," said his Aunt with a big smile on her face.

"What's that?" said the boy now turning his attention away from the television to his aunt.

"Well, I like you and I want to do something to you that girls who like boys do to boys. It's the job of girls to do it to boys. It will feel really good."

"Ok," the boy slowly responded.

"In order for me to do it, you have to promise not to tell anybody. If you ever tell anyone, you'll never be able to come here again. You understand."

"Sure. I understand. I won't tell anyone. I swear."

"Cross your heart and hope to die?"

"Yes. I won't say anything; cross my heart and hope to die."

"Alright then. Pull down your pants and let me show you what girls do to boys that they like."

The boy stood up and hesitantly pulled his shorts and underwear down. His aunt reached for his penis and started fondling him. With her hand making him erect, he realized that she was telling the truth it did feel good. He felt quite weird about what was going on but he also didn't want it to stop.

"Sit on the couch," his Aunt Sheila said.

Once he had sat back down his aunt got onto her knees and took her nephew's penis into her mouth. He liked this even more than he liked her hand. Simultaneously, he felt even weirder and didn't know what to make of why his aunt wanted to do this to him. This first time she performed this act of fellatio on him for what seemed like forever before finishing up by giving him a kiss on the cheek and reminding him of his promise not to tell anyone and that women and girls were supposed to do this.

Of course, he never told a soul because he was concerned with not being able to visit his cousin and best friend Lucas as well as his eight year old reasoning of what was so wrong with his Aunt Sheila doing what girls do to boys they like to him. It couldn't hurt anyone. Over the rest of the summer, his aunt found opportunities to get some alone time with her nephew and performed the same sex act on him dozens of times.

As the years went by and he visited cousin Lucas every summer, the two of them progressed from oral sex to sexual intercourse. All the while, his aunt indoctrinated him with the notion that women should always be willing to pleasure men in this way without question. At the age of thirteen, the ball-capped man was completely engulfed in performing these acts with his aunt. Even when they visited for his Uncle James' funeral, they both found the time to get together in the morning before the event and pleasure each other.

The ball-capped man slowly snapped out of his reminiscent daydream and realized that he had a tight grip on Hilda while remembering the good times with his Aunt Sheila. Smiling he kissed Hilda on the cheek before getting up and reattaching her restraints. Exhausted and drugged, Hilda was in a deep sleep.

CHAPTER 4

After canvassing the local registered sex offender population and confirming that they all had sufficient alibis, Detective Wilson Riley and his partner, Irene Rands, were back to square one in their investigation. Riley sat alone staring at the photographs of the four women who had been kidnapped, raped, and released in Olympia in as many months and wondered if they would ever catch the son-of-a-bitch who was responsible. The images showed them in various stages of distress and sadness. Some were distraught and sobbing others with melancholic somber looks on their faces. They moved Riley at his very core. They motivated him to work overtime to find the perpetrator. After all, this was why he had become a police officer in the first place; he wanted to help people. He wanted to protect people. Hell, he wanted to give the victims of crimes some form of solace and vengeance.

Wilson Riley had grown up in Seattle's Central District neighborhood and seen criminals victimize its' working class people. Many of the police officers he saw in his neighborhood had been white and there didn't seem to be much in the way of good relations between the Seattle Police Department and the black people in his community. This is what led to him joining the ranks of law enforcement. He wanted to fight crime and put a face on law enforcement that would reach out to the black community. He knew that black people didn't enjoy having criminals among them but that they also didn't appreciate having police treat every black person in a community as if they were all criminals. Whether it was pimps forcing women to sell their bodies against their wills or drug dealers scaring people who complained about them selling drugs in front of their homes or recruiting children to be mules for their drugs, Riley had seen it all and he abhorred it. He wanted to do something about it. Ever since he graduated from the Western Washington University, he had his mind made up to become a police officer. He applied with every police agency with an opening. After competing for several dozen job openings with a variety of police agencies, Wilson finally got hired by the Olympia Police Department. This is where he spent the last fifteen years of his career, eleven of which have been with the department's Sex Crimes Unit.

He sat rummaging through boxes of evidence on his desk related to the four rapes that they were now investigating. Riley hoped that he had overlooked something that would provide a clue that could give them a lead but he had his doubts because he had gone through these boxes too many times to count. However, at this point Riley was willing to do anything to catch the vile son-of-a-bitch who was committing these rapes.

His longtime partner, Irene Rands, came into the room. Rands was a short slightly overweight redhead who generally avoided the sun because of her extremely fair skin. It gave her somewhat of a ghostly appearance but she substantially reduced her risk of developing skin cancer, which made her feel great. Both suffering from long dry spells in the romance department, Riley and Rands threw themselves into catching sex offenders. Putting in extra hours to solve cases. Getting commendations from the Olympia Police Department brass for their job performance.

"Riley, we've got another missing woman. She's possibly number five for the serial rapist were looking for because of the sudden way in which she vanished. Her fiancé reported her missing this morning when he went to pick her up at her apartment and she wasn't there."

"Damn! Not again," frowned Riley lurching forward in his seat.

"Yeah, I know. We've got to stop this monster," Rands said.

"What do we know about her?" asked Riley rising from his seat.

"She's a white female, age thirty-two, attorney, and engaged to be married later this year."

"So there is no pattern with this fucking guy at all. Damn it!"

"Not at all, we have a twenty-five year old gas station clerk, a forty year old stay-at-home mom, a forty-eight year old doctor, a twenty-two year old secretary, and a thirty-nine year old bus driver."

"Add to that a thirty-two year old attorney. And nothing about any of them is the same. Not their hair color, lifestyle, or eye color. I guess the one similarity is that they are all white women."

"So what made this bastard target these women?"

"Maybe he just simply hates women."

"That's definitely a possibility. Look at all the crazy shit he's written on their bodies using permanent markers," Rands said pointing to the board filled with photographs, a map, and other items collected in their investigation with as a chill ran up her spine. "He's absolutely got issues with members of the opposite sex. And what the fuck does he mean by 'Deregulate Rape,' 'Sex is not a Crime,' 'Repeal RCW 9A.44.050,' 'Pussy is Every Man's Right' 'Restore manhood'…this guy is one sick motherfucker."

"I know he is and we've got a lot of ground to cover to answer the question about what made him target these women so we can stop him from attacking anyone else. If he was as neat as the last four times there's not likely to be any evidence of his crimes to help us get any closer to catching him. Let's go interview her fiancé, co-workers, and friends to see if they noticed anything strange before she disappeared," said Riley as he took a swig of stale coffee and contemplated spitting it back into the cup before finally choking it down as they walked out of the office.

Riley and Rands knocked on the door hard several times before a thin man with a neatly trimmed beard answered the door. His face bore a panicked look.

"My name is Detective Irene Rands and this is my partner Detective Wilson Riley. We're here to see Steve Roy."

"I'm Steve. Did you find her?" he said with a hopeful look starting to appear on his face.

"No sir. We're here to ask you a few questions to help us investigate her disappearance."

"Oh ok," Steve responded disappointedly. He had a large lump in his stomach that started to rise into his throat. Steve felt sick.

"Can we come in?" Riley asked.

"Oh yes. Sorry for being rude. Come in. I'm just a little distracted right now with Hilda being missing and all," stepping back inside and holding the door for Riley and Rands to come in.

Being detectives, Riley and Rands both scanned the room. It's a habit that seasoned law enforcement officers have that's hard to break in addition to the fact that they hadn't yet cleared Steve as a suspect.

"Please have a seat," offered Steve gesturing toward his couch. "Can I offer you guys something the drink?"

"No thanks. We won't take too much of your time Mr. Roy. We just have a few questions," Rands said.

"Call me Steve."

"When did you last see Hilda?"

"Last Friday. That was two days before I went to her apartment to pick her up. She had a big case she was working on and planned to spend most of the weekend on it."

"What about any other contact with her? Any text messages, e-mail, or phone calls?"

"Nope because when she's preparing for trial she needs her space. I have to respect her needs."

"I understand that."

"Has she ever taken off on her own without telling anyone?" asked

Riley.

"No. Never. She's very responsible and would never shirk off something as important as a trial. Hell, she loves going to trial. It's…like…what she does for fun."

"Do you have a current photograph of her that we can have?"

"Oh yes, I thought you guys would ask for one. Take this one," Steve frantically said handing Riley a photograph that had been on the coffee table. "It's the most recent one I have. Do you think she's been taken by the serial rapist? Is there anything I can do to help?"

"We don't know what has happened to her at this time. We'll work hard to find her. You've helped us out quite a bit."

Riley and Rands both stood up, shook hands with Steve, and thanked him for his cooperation before exiting Steve's place. They both realized that Hilda was most likely a victim of the serial rapist that they had been pursuing in all the other rape cases but there was no way to know for sure until she turned up again like all of the other victims.

Steve didn't know what to do. He was lost in this moment. The woman that he loved was missing and he couldn't do a damn thing about it. Calling the police felt like nothing. He didn't gain any solace from the encounter with them. The helplessness he felt earlier when he couldn't find her at her place or her office seemed to have taking root deep in him. He couldn't eat. All he wanted to do was sit on the couch and stare at the wall and wait for her to call, walk through the door, or something.

CHAPTER 5

Annie parked her car on Legion Way near the old State Department of Personnel building. She grabbed her purse and started walking toward the intersection of Legion Way and Franklin Street worried that she would be late for her meeting with her CCO. It was the standard south Puget Sound day, drizzle. She crossed the street and stumbled a bit when she stepped up onto the curb on account of her ridiculously large feet getting hung up on it. Regaining her balance she continued on toward the corner of Legion Way and Capitol Way toward a local coffee shop but as she passed an alley she heard a faint sound, almost like a wounded animal. Pausing for a moment and backing up, Annie listened but didn't hear it again. As soon as she started walking again, she heard the same faint sound. She couldn't quite make out what the sound was but was disturbed by it.

Annie reversed course and went into the alley slowly moving toward the weak sound she had heard where she saw a pair of fairly new athletic shoes sticking from behind a large furniture box. The shoes contained a pair of feet and legs that were obstructed by the box. Annie's heart began pounding at the thought of what might be behind the box. Her mind immediately thought that she had come upon a dead body. Annie slowly approached the box and peeped around it to see a woman lying on the ground in athletic apparel. Her eyes were partially shut and she appeared to be very lethargic but alive. As Annie rushed to help the woman she saw that the woman had "Fuck Hole" scrawled onto her forehead along with "Cum Guzzler" and "Anal Queen" on her left and right arms respectively.

Her upper chest also bore the word "Catch and Release." Annie saw various other obscene and insulting phrases written all over the woman.

"Oh, my God! Are you alright? What happened?" shouted Annie trying to left the woman to the sitting position.

"I was…I was," squeaked the woman as she began to lose consciousness.

"You were what?" asked Annie. Annie tried to wake the woman. "You were what?"

"Raped," whispered the woman as she lost consciousness.

After rolling the woman carefully onto her back, Annie took out her cell phone and rapidly dialed 9-1-1.

"9-1-1, what's your emergency?" asked the female dispatcher.

"Hey, I found a woman lying in an alley here on…on…Legion. We need an ambulance and the police.

"Ma'am where are you on Legion?"

"Umm, behind the Best Drip Coffee on Legion. Oh, and she told me she's been raped."

"The police and ambulance are on their way."

"What's your name?"

"It's Annie Lone."

There was a long pause. "Are you the Annie Lone who saved the women at the prison?"

"Yes, that's me," responded Annie feeling a little awkward about the question.

"Wow, I just want to tell you how much you inspire me."

"Uh, thank you," said Annie feeling even more awkward because of the current situation.

"Anyway, just sit tight they'll be their shortly. When they get there you may hang up. You think you could come down to dispatch one day to meet me and the girls?"

"Have you seen my website?"

"Yes," crowed the dispatcher.

"Okay, then send me an e-mail through the website and I'll see what I can…sorry I see the police car I've got to go."

"Okay, thank you Annie," said the jovial 9-1-1 dispatcher.

"Officer, she's over here," yelled Annie as she waved the police officer toward her direction.

The ambulance arrived shortly thereafter and two EMTs emerged from the vehicle, one male and one female. They both proceeded immediately toward the unconscious woman on the ground and began looking her over for injuries while the uniformed police officer began interviewing Annie about her observations. All that Annie could think of after seeing the vulnerable woman lying on the ground was this had to be the work of the serial rapist her mother told her about this morning.

The female EMT started attaching a blood pressure cuff to the barely conscious woman's arm.

"Ma'am, what's your name," said the female EMT. "Can you hear me ma'am?"

"Yes I can hear you," the woman whispered. "Hilda. My name's Hilda Bell. He attacked me."

The officer talking to Annie immediately interrupted her mid-answer and turned his attention to the Hilda.

"Miss, I heard you say that he attacked you. Do you know his name?" said the officer.

"No, I don't know him."

"Do you remember what he looked like?"

"I couldn't see his face," Hilda dizzily shook her head.

The female EMT cut the officer off before he could ask another question.

"Let us finish assessing her injuries and then you can talk to her," grunted the female EMT.

The officer nodded his agreement and turned his attention back to Annie.

"Did you see anybody else in the alley when you found her?" said the officer.

"No, I didn't see anyone."

As the officer continued questioning Annie, her thoughts were of the poor woman lying on the ground. She couldn't focus on the questions the officer asked her. She worried about what had happened to Hilda. She stared at Hilda as the EMTs worked to prepare her for the trip to the emergency room. As they did, Hilda was becoming more and more aware of her surroundings. She frantically asked for her fiancé while the EMTs tried to calm her down. Hilda's questions became louder and more hysterical. She was in a state of despair.

This reminded Annie of how distraught Sibyl was after her own attack when they were in prison. Annie's heart sank as she thought of Hilda going through the same trauma. Sibyl's rape had nearly destroyed her life. Annie struggled to regain her focus on what the officer was asking. As the EMTs placed Hilda on the gurney, a local news van arrived and the female reporter quickly exited the van and rushed the driver-cameraman to get his camera going. But before he could get setup the EMTs loaded Hilda into the back of the ambulance to head to the emergency room.

After getting the call and driving across town with their lights on and siren blaring, Riley and Rands walked into the emergency room with somber looks on their faces at the realization that the woman whose fiancé that they had just met with was now in the hospital. What they learned from the dispatcher was that the rapist had dumped her in an alley like a piece of garbage. They were also more concerned than ever because of the serial rapist's victim count was increasing and they felt helpless to stop him as none of the prior investigations had turned up even a shred of useful evidence to identify the monster other than a white male with a ball-cap on and his psychopathic writings about sex and women. Riley and Rands entered the emergency room cursorily extending their badges at the security desk and being immediately pointed in the direction of Exam Room 3 where a uniformed officer stood as a sentinel outside the door. Riley and Rands both quietly entered the room as the nurse finished changing Hilda's IV. Hilda looked extremely distressed lying in bed.

"Ms. Bell, I'm Detective Irene Rands of the Olympia Police Department. This is my partner Detective Wilson Riley. We're trying to find out what happened to you. Can you answer a few questions for us?"

"Yes," Hilda responded in a low voice.

"Can you tell us how you got into the alley?"

"No, I can't," said Hilda with her eyes fixed on her entwined hands. "I guess…I mean. I don't remember."

"What's the last thing you remember?"

"I remember this creepy son-of-a-bitch wearing a ball cap raping me," Hilda replied with a few tears in her eyes.

"Any details about his body that you can recall that might help us identify him?"

"No, he had the lighting too low for me to see his face or if he had any tattoos or anything," Hilda cried while tears began streaming down her cheeks.

"Do you remember anything that stood out about the place where you were held?"

"Only that he had a whiteboard that talked about rape not being illegal and other sick shit," said Hilda, growing more agitated as signaled by her shaking hand. "It seemed that I was in a basement because he came down a flight of stairs."

Riley wrote a note about this flight of stairs in his investigation notebook after he and Rands glanced at each other quickly. Despite their best efforts, Hilda noticed them.

"What? What's significant about that?" Hilda asked with a ray of hope in her voice despite her face being covered in tears.

"It's the first time we've heard of a flight of stairs," added Riley.

"Is it a big break?" Hilda cried.

"It's too soon to tell but it's good that you noticed this," added Rands.

"We understand that you're a lawyer here in town. What kind of cases do you handle?" asked Riley.

"Primarily employment litigation and personal injury. I don't handle any criminal cases."

"Any dissatisfied clients or opposing parties that were unusually upset with your work or threatening?"

"No, not really. Nothing that stands out as unusual."

"So you didn't see anything about his body that would help you pick him out from a group of strangers," continued Riley.

"No."

"Did he say anything to you?"

"He just let me know that he was in control and that nothing I did to resist would stop him. He even told me that he'd like it if I fought back," Hilda trying to stifle herself from openly sobbing.

"Would you be able to identify him by his voice?"

"Yes. Oh, God yes! His creepy, nattering voice will be with me for the rest of my life," said Hilda as she pulled her sheets up around her neck in a protective manner. "I keep hearing him say those things to me over and over again."

"Anything else stand out in your mind that you think will help us make an arrest?"

"Well, he doesn't seem to think that you'll be able to catch him. Even though he never used condoms he thoroughly…excuse me," sobbed Hilda as her crying became uncontrollable with the terrible memories flooding her mind with no end in sight. Her thoughts went right back to the question of why. Why would he ruin her life like this? Hilda couldn't wrap her mind around it and it tore her apart inside. All she could think was why. It consumed her right there in that moment as the detectives questioned her.

"We can come back and finish up later if you want Ms. Bell," asked Rands.

"No, I've got to do this," sputtered Hilda wiping tears from her eyes as she tried to pull herself together. "He can't be allowed to get away with this. He cleaned me up after when I was unconscious so there would be no DNA evidence."

Seeing that Hilda was starting to fall apart after thinking about the ball-capped rapist doing things to her while she was unconscious, Rands decided to wrap up the interview.

"Thank you Ms. Bell. You've been very helpful. Here's my card, if anything comes up that you want to talk about don't hesitate to call me. No matter what it is," Rands said before she and Riley left the room. As they walked out of the room a man quickly passed them on his way into Exam Room 3.

"Steve! I love you," Hilda said loudly as the man sat down on the bed and embraced her.

"I love you too. I'm here for you," asked Steve.

Riley and Rands were relieved to hear that Hilda had someone there for her. They knew that this would be one of the most difficult moments in her life and felt better that she wouldn't have to do it alone.

CHAPTER 6

Annie walked through the double doors of the Olympia Community Corrections Field Office to meet with her CCO. The central lobby of the field office was large with several rows of chairs that had been bolted down to the floor. The lobby had a damp musty smell permeating throughout it mixed with a slightly nauseating smell of body odor. There were several people waiting in the lobby; some with small children.

Annie felt uncomfortable every time she came into this office. This time was no different. One guy sat in a corner and stared at her with a creepy leering look. From the time she checked in with the receptionist to the point she sat down, his eerie gaze followed her and never broke off. Another man sat with his girlfriend in the back row of the seats and argued in low voices about money from what Annie could make out. He seemed very angry but his girlfriend didn't back down as their argument droned on. Annie took a seat near the secured door as she waited for her CCO to come get her.

As a term of her conditional pardon, Annie had to report to a CCO for one year after her release from prison for her conditional pardon to convert into a full pardon. Dozens of these offices were operated by the Washington State Department of Corrections as central locations for offenders to meet with their CCOs who check on their compliance with the terms and conditions of community supervision. CCOs were responsible for making sure that offenders received the services they needed whether it was mental health treatment, chemical dependency programs, anger management classes, or sex offender treatment just to name a few. CCOs were also responsible for conducting urinalysis (UA) exams to make sure that offenders were not using alcohol or drugs. In addition to that, CCOs also had to make sure that offenders maintained jobs or went to school, reported changes of their addresses, and got permission before leaving their county or the state. If Annie or any of the other offenders violated any of these conditions, they could be arrested by the CCOs and punished with short stints of incarceration or other penalty sanction designed to gain their compliance.

Annie was not your average offender. Generally, offenders who reported to Community Corrections Field Offices were either released from prison after serving their sentences or those who had been convicted of certain misdemeanors in state superior courts. Annie was pardoned; conditionally pardoned but pardoned nonetheless. This meant that she would report to a CCO for a set period of time and her conviction would be entirely expunged from the record because the Governor had the constitutional power to do so.

As Annie sat waiting, the lobby quickly filled with offenders, their moms, wives, husbands, girlfriends, boyfriends, and children. A line quickly formed in front of a young woman who sat behind a counter protected by bulletproof glass. She took the name of each offender and made sure that the CCO responsible for supervising that offender knew that the offender had arrived for their meeting. Occasionally, a CCO would open a secure door and call the name of an offender who would be taken back to an office to meet. They would discuss the offender's progress for about ten to fifteen minutes. Sometimes the CCO would have to arrest the offender for failing to report at predetermined times, not going to required treatment programs, testing positive for drugs on a urinalysis, or any number of other reasons. In those cases, the CCO would get permission from the Community Corrections Supervisor of his office to make the arrest and coordinate it with fellow CCOs to assist in taking the offender into custody and transporting the offender to either a violator facility (usually a county jail under contract) or a prison. Annie was lucky on this day because she didn't have to witness an arrest, which could be either unremarkable or extremely violent.

When the offenders hadn't complied with rules and requirements of their sentence, the CCOs would have to place them in custody. Some of the offenders didn't want to go to back to jail so they would put up a fight as multiple CCOs tried to restrain them and place them in handcuffs. Punches would be thrown and control techniques would be applied with the end result of someone suffering some minor, if not, serious injury. Annie hated being in the field office when that happened.

As she sat waiting for her turn to meet with her CCO, Annie's thoughts returned to the young woman she found in the alley. Ever since her incarceration in prison, Annie's empathy for women who suffered from sexual violence had grown exponentially. It grew to a point that it almost became a personal mission for her to try and stamp out violence against women. Even as she suffered her own sexual violence at the hands of her late husband Billy, Annie never really thought about how others were affected by rape. Her short stay at Mount Baker Corrections Center for Women brought everything into sharp focus. Seeing her best friend Sibyl being brutally raped and watching the video of the torture and murder of Jessica Wick made Annie fully aware of these issues. Now she focused on this woman in the same way and wanted to help her. She wanted to get justice for her. She wanted her not to live in fear of this animal coming after her again or relishing his attack on her. She wanted to cut his rancid dick off.

After about thirty minutes, a fifty-two year old woman poked her head from behind the secure door.

"Come on back Annie," said McKenzie Vonde, Annie's CCO. Vonde was a no nonsense person. Even though she was one of the armed CCOs who worked for DOC, she did not use her position of power to intimidate offenders. She simply told offenders her expectations and informed them that she would arrest them if they did not comply with those expectations including those set by the court. She also explained to them that she would do all she could within her power to help them succeed at whatever they wanted to achieve. Vonde's track record of success was extensive including several chefs graduating culinary schools (one opening his own restaurant in Vancouver, Washington), an offender who opened a construction firm, as well as several nurses. She also worked with drug addicted women through a local shelter to get them clean and back on track with their lives. After fifteen years, she had helped twenty-eight women. None of them had fallen off the wagon. All of them had graduated from college. All of them had stable relationships.

Annie and Vonde had not met in a month and a half now and they had some catching up to do. Annie stood up and walked toward the door held open by Vonde.

"Good morning, CCO Vonde."

"Morning Annie."

Annie followed Vonde down a long narrow hall to a corner office that had bare walls and were painted an off-white color. Once inside, Annie sat in a chair facing a small desk while Vonde shut the door behind them.

"What's new?" asked Vonde.

"Not much."

"Good. That means soon enough your pardon will become permanent."

"Hold on. I guess I should tell you that I had to call the cops this morning."

"Oh, why?"

"I found a woman behind Best Drip Coffee lying on the ground with all kinds of writing on her body. The writing was quite vulgar. She said she had been raped."

"Well, that's alright...I mean it's alright that you called the police. I had thought you were into something else."

"Nope."

"I do hope that the lady is okay."

"Me too. I'm so worried about her. I just wish I could do

something for her."

"Like what?"

"Well, I don't know."

"Let me just tell you. Everything is going great for you now. I'm fully aware of what you did at the women's prison and find it commendable but don't go and throw yourself in the middle of something that could jeopardize everything you have now. The Oly PD is more than capable of helping this woman."

"Yea, I know," replied Annie.

As the meeting continued, Annie thought to herself that the Olympia Police weren't doing that great a job. This woman appeared to be the fifth victim of the serial rapist. She understood that she couldn't jeopardize her pardon by trying to become some type of vigilante but there must be something that she could do within the confines of the law to help. While Vonde continued going through her files and asking her questions, Annie's mind seemed to be fixated on the wellbeing of the stranger she found on her way to this meeting.

CHAPTER 7

"Dylan! Come on in. It's almost nap time," said Allison, holding the door to the mud room open for the boy to come in from the garage. Frustrated by the closing garage door, the ball-capped man who had been kneeling down behind a row of garbage cans slowly crept around the back of the house looking for a window for a good view of Allison. Spotting a large greenbelt just behind the house, the ball-capped man quickly found a tree that was suitable to climb and clumsily clambered up it near the top for a view into the house. He had a direct view into the master bedroom. As he sat there staring through a window into an empty bedroom, he remembered the most important intimate sexual encounter of his life.

He was only fourteen years old. He walked down the dark hallway and opened the door to her bedroom. Climbing into bed, the ball-capped man, then a boy, removed his underwear and slowly started massaging the woman's breasts as she lay with her back to him. She became aroused by his touch and woke up.

"Harry, I see you're home and happy to see me," she said in the dark bedroom as she rolled over and started stroking the boy's now hard cock.

Saying nothing, the boy climbed on top of her, inserted his cock into her, and started pumping in and out. The woman reached up, pulled his face toward her to kiss him, but noticed that there wasn't any facial hair. She reached onto the night stand, turned on the light, and saw her own son on top of her.

"What are you doing? Get off me!" his mother said angrily.

"No mom, I need to do this," declared the fourteen year old. "We need this."

"No...Don't! Stop! Get off! Adam, stop!" shouted his mother, feverishly struggling to get him out of, and off of, her but there was no use. The fourteen year old boy who stood at 5'10" had grown to become stronger than his mother.

"Mom, this is for your own good. This is for us."

"I thought you were Harry. Get off me now," yelled his mother.

"Harry isn't good enough for you. I love you, mom."

"I love you too but not this way. Please stop," cried his mother.

The boy continued pumping in and out of his mother until he let out a loud grunt and collapsed on top of her.

His mother started to sob uncontrollably. She just cried a loud disappointed cry while the boy continued to lay on top of her breathing heavily.

"What are you crying for?" asked the boy, sounding a little bewildered.

"This isn't right."

"The hell it isn't. We're going to be together forever. You and me."

"I'm your mother. This is unnatural. We can't..."

"Shhh. Our love is all that matters, mom."

Three weeks after her son forced himself on her, his mother took her own life using Harry's gun. She didn't leave a note or anything else indicating why she had done it but the boy knew. He knew that they had conceived a child that night. He knew because he watched his mother closely and had timed their sexual encounter to take place soon after her period. A few weeks later his belief was confirmed when he found the discarded pregnancy test in the garbage and he knew that Harry had had a vasectomy years earlier.

The ball-capped man looked back on this memory with fondness and sadness. He was fond of the *relationship* that had developed between him and his mother. He was sad because she never carried his child to full term so that he could see the baby come from the same fertile soil from which he had also risen. The ball-capped man snapped out of his thought when Allison entered her bedroom.

She immediately turned on the baby monitor to hear the child. Allison sat on the edge of the bed for a minute and sighed. It was only just after noon but it seemed like a full day with the child. Those kids had her frazzled. Finally, she had a minute to herself. A chance to relax and unwind. She stood and started undressing and went into the master bathroom where she remained for about ten minutes. She came back into the room wearing only a robe. She picked up a photograph of her and her husband sitting on the table next to the bed and just stared at it with a smile on her face. He was a very handsome man. She thought he was downright hot. Just as hot as she thought he was when they first met. From looking at the photo and her thoughts of his attractiveness, Allison became quit aroused.

It had been two weeks since they were last intimate; two long weeks since he last put his arms around her and pulled her close. She remembered how good it was when he did. She listened to the monitor and didn't hear a peep out of the twins and in that moment decided to give herself a little release. Allison scooted back on the bed against the headboard, placed the photo back on the table, and reached down between her legs. Closing her eyes, Allison began softly and slowly massaging her clitoris. It was electric, the pleasure she felt from her efforts. The more she thought of his hands caressing her, the more she became engulfed in the heat of the moment. The arousal spread over her like a warm flood of water. Her mind wandered to the time her husband placed his mouth there. From head to toe, the erotic arousal engulfed every fiber of her being until it started to overflow. Using her freehand, she massaged and played with her nipples, which were hyper-stimulated. With her head thrown back over the pillow in deep ecstasy, she began grinding her hips intensely against her hand.

Still perched precariously in the tree ogling Allison through the window, the ball-capped man had pushed his jeans and underwear down to just above his knees and was frantically stroking his penis until he lost control. His semen wound up in his underwear and on the tree. As a squirrel stopped on a nearby branch and gawked at him, he felt a little awkward and waved to the animal to leave but it just sat there staring. He didn't like the squirrel watching him. It made him feel uncomfortable. As if his privacy was being violated. His attention went back to the window where he saw that Allison had finished and was now lying under the covers about to go to sleep. The ball-capped man pulled his underwear and pants up. There was no doubt about it now. He knew he had to have this woman. He started thinking about his recon mission on her. He had so much to learn about her. He couldn't let his desire to have her alter his usual well-thought out approach to acquiring her. After carefully managing to climb down from his insidious perch, he immediately thought about the execution of his plan.

He stumbled through the greenbelt making his way back to his car with an air of excitement engulfing him. He had so many questions rolling around in his head that needed answering. Were there any guns in the house? There was an air of excitement around him. Here was the perfect woman before him. She obviously had a strong sexual appetite and he wanted to be the one to satisfy her desires. He wanted her to be that special lady to give him all the things that his life was missing.

The first time he saw Allison was love at first sight. She wore a lovely sundress that made her seem like the most elegant woman. The way she glided down Percival Landing pushing the stroller made his heart melt. He felt an instant connection with her. It was in that instant that he understood his unquenchable desire to have her as his own.

CHAPTER 8

The security gate slowly rolled open as Hannah Jane emerged from behind it and started toward the blue sedan parked in the visitor area. Two women came out of the parked car and ran toward Hannah Jane. It was Annie and Sibyl. They both embraced her hard.

"My God! It's so good to see you Hannah Jane," shouted Sibyl as she tightly squeezed her.

"You too," Hannah Jane replied, trying to resist smiling.

"Hannah Jane, your hair is so long…and beautiful," said Annie, pulling Hannah Jane's hair out of her mouth as the hug between them ended.

Hannah Jane had been in prison for a long time and, up to now, couldn't imagine what she would do outside of prison. Here she was forty-six years old with no real plans of what to do with herself. Since meeting Annie in prison, Hannah Jane had worked hard on controlling her anger. With the help of her prison mental health counselor, she had begun to realize that much of her anger stemmed from her father's participation in her rape when she was just fifteen years old. She remembered like it was yesterday.

When she yelled for his help, he came and discovered two of his drinking buddies tearing away at her clothing and rather than killing the sons of bitches, he joined in and forced her to perform every degrading sexual act that the three degenerate assholes could think of forcing her to do. Lacking any sense of security or self-esteem, Hannah Jane developed a nearly impenetrable emotional defensive shell. She refused to care about anyone because she didn't believe that anyone else could truly care about her. Her scars were reflected in her anger, rage, and inability to connect with anyone else. Meeting Annie and Sibyl changed all that. She had real friends; friends who did love her. She couldn't quite comprehend that but she accepted and tried to return that love to them.

"Thank you both. Anybody looking at us would think we were some kind of lesbian triple threat," Hannah Jane joked, with her usual crass sense of humor. "Seriously, Annie, thank you for giving me a place to stay while I get on my feet."

"Hey don't mention it. Life's about being there for the people you care about," said Annie.

The normally rough and tough Hannah Jane teared up. "Don't do that Hannah Jane. It's not that big of a deal," added Annie pulling out a tissue and dabbing Hannah Jane's eyes.

"I've never had anyone be there for me is all. It's not something I'm used to."

"Well, we love you. You're like our sister. You're stuck with us forever."

"That's right Hannah Jane," said Sibyl.

"I love you two bitches too."

"That sounds like the Hannah Jane we know. So let's get away from this prison," Annie said.

"Where can a girl get a decent meal around here?" asked Hannah Jane.

"I know just the place. Let's go," Sibyl replied.

As the three women piled into the car, the tower officers of Mount Baker Corrections Center for Women looked on with smiles as they saw the two women responsible for cleaning up MBCCW, Annie and Hannah Jane, reunited.

Hannah Jane sat in the back seat a little taken aback by the warm welcome she had received from Annie and Sibyl. People from her background rarely experienced true love. Not romantic love but love. It's a hard thing to come by in friendships. It's hard to trust. It's hard to express caring and concern for strangers who often think, in our modern society, that the person expressing it is seeking something in return. But Annie and Sibyl only sought her friendship in return. Hannah Jane felt the love of friendship as the car trundled down the gravel road away from the prison. She fully understood that this was love. This was true friendship. Love generated by friendship is absolutely the best.

At the restaurant the ladies talked for hours. They reminisced about the few and far between good times that they had at MBCCW. They also talked about Annie's newfound fame as an activist for women's rights. Finally, their conversation turned to Hannah Jane's plans.

"I'm not too sure what it is I want to do but what I do know is that I want to do something to help you Annie," Hannah Jane said.

"Well, of course you can. I'm sure at some point though you'll come up with something that interests you," said Annie.

"Yeah maybe but for the mean time I'll do my best to help you so that I'm not too much of a moocher."

"You can never be a moocher Hannah Jane," smiled Annie. "You're one of our best friends. Right Sibyl?"

"Heck yeah," grinned Sibyl. "We're a team."

"Tell me about Olympia. I've never spent much time there. I only passed through in the past," asked Hannah Jane.

"It's a nice little town with very few problems. Well, right now in Oly there's some sick bastard kidnapping women, raping them, and releasing them. The police don't have a clue as to who he is and not a shred of evidence," Annie explained.

"These assholes are all over the place aren't they?"

"I guess there are just men in this world who feel a sense of entitlement. They think that they can do whatever they want."

"Are you doing anything to catch this sick fucker?"

"No but I really want to do something to help. Too many women have already been attacked."

"What are you waiting for? Let's catch this douche bag."

"My CCO warned me against getting involved. She said my pardon is set to become permanent soon and I don't need anything to happen that may interfere with it."

"I understand Annie but dammit we can't just sit on our hands while these women keep getting attacked. Can we? You convinced me at the prison that we needed to stand up for other women and I'll be damned if I don't do something to help."

"You're right Hannah Jane. I'll figure out something that we can do to help. Give me some time to think about it. In the meantime, we better hit the road to head home. It's getting dark."

CHAPTER 9

The ball-capped man sat on the floor in his basement sanctuary going through a bag of garbage wearing a surgical mask. With gloves on, he fumbled with the smelly refuse as he picked through it. Taking pieces from the pile and tossing them into the garbage bag lying next to him, he slowly and methodically navigated his way through the broad sea of filth. Now, he knew her name was Allison Silson because he had located a few scraps of garbage that he had set aside with her name on them but he needed to know more. He wanted to know her. He wanted to get lost in her and everything that she was. What was her favorite food? What was her favorite color? What type of guy did she like; the strong silent type or outgoing? You know the important things that help you identify with a woman. The pile began dwindling down to only a few pieces of trash when the ball-capped man began to panic. He wasn't finding what he was looking for in the pile. Now he realized that he had to go into her house, which he didn't like to do but understood was sometimes necessary to achieve his goal.

Feeling his anxiety growing about having to go into the house, he tried to calm himself. He understood that it was a necessary part of his ultimate goal but every time he had to do it he felt nervous. One of the things he often did to calm down was to think of happier times. Then he remembered something from a couple of weeks earlier. He had recently seen a woman that instantly drew his interest. She was absolutely beautiful. He didn't know anything about her. He had only taken quick glances in her direction the one or two times he had been in her presence. She intimidated him but he thought this was good. The way she carried herself was with quiet confidence as well as strength. Yet there was a strong air of femininity oozing from her every movement that caused him to become extremely aroused in her presence. Fully intrigued by this woman, he wanted to meet her. He longed to talk to her. How could a schlub like him approach a goddess like her? As his mind drifted over the images of this woman in his head an alarm clock began buzzing loudly, which caused him to snap out of the trance that had engulfed him.

He jumped from his seated position on the floor and quickly started rushing around because he would be late if he didn't get a move on right away. He needed to get to Allison's house quickly so that he could observe her every movement to plan for getting together with her. He had to focus his mind. He could meet this other captivating woman some other time. Right now he needed to get in place so that he could learn as much as he could about Allison. His heart pounded. He only had a short window of time to get in place. If he was even a little late, he might either be seen by Allison, her husband, or her neighbors. He longed to live and breathe Allison. She was perfect. The woman that he knew would give him exactly what he wanted.

As he packed the final items he needed into his backpack, the ball-capped man stood up and rushed out the front door. Fully engaged in his thoughts about how wonderful Allison would be and how she would be the one who would fulfill his dreams, he only had to finish laying all the ground work to make it a reality.

CHAPTER 10

Annie walked into the Olympia Police Station in the Olympia City Hall on Fourth Avenue and immediately put down her umbrella and shook as much water off of it as possible. It was quite a stunning building; a substantial improvement over the old city hall, which looked like a pretentious architect's serious lack of creativity. Anyway, the new city hall was a fabulous new addition to the city.

Annie walked up to the main reception counter and asked, "Can I see someone who investigates sex crimes?"

"Do you have a specific case number?" asked the receptionist.

"It's regarding the serial rapist running around Olympia," replied Annie.

"That's Detectives Wilson Riley and Irene Rands. Hold on, I'll see if they are available."

While she was waiting Annie looked around the expansive lobby and people-watched. She saw the worthless Olympia Mayor Bill Stopins pass through the lobby as if he was God's gift to the world when the guy could barely tie his own shoes. However, he was mayor as christened by his ability to hit baseballs in high school and college not because of his deep intellect or policy proposals; goes to show you that American elections have become nothing more than high-priced popularity contests based on the best sound bite deliverer or biggest celebrity. The guy spends more time on the golf course rather than doing the business of mayor.

"Detective Riley will be down to see you in a minute. You can have a seat over there," the receptionist announced pointing to the bench near a large potted plant.

Annie took a seat but no sooner than she sat down did a Black man standing about six foot, five inches tall wearing a sweatshirt that said "Western Washington University" on it with a badge on a lanyard hanging around his neck and gun in a shoulder holster rounded a corner and headed directly toward her. He was a very handsome fellow with a well-defined outline of his biceps bulging through the somewhat tight sweatshirt sleeves. The man extended his right hand toward Annie and said, "I'm Detective Wilson Riley. What's up?"

"Well, Detective Riley I…"

"Call me Wilson," smiled Riley.

"O…Okay. I came down here to find out if there was anything that us locals could do to assist you in tracking down this serial rapist," Annie nervously said. She was attracted to Detective Riley and tried not to betray her unforeseen attraction to this man. She had never even considered dating a black man before and now here she was anxiously trying to talk to this man without seeming like she was coming on to him.

Trying to conceal his own interest in her and appear professional Riley said, "I don't think I caught your name."

"Annie Lone," she said.

"You're the lady who freed the inmates at Mount Baker, right?"

"Right, I just want you guys to know that if you want any assistance I'm willing to step up to the plate and help organize the local community to catch this guy."

"Thank you Annie but I think we can handle it. All of my time is focused on catching this creep."

Feeling a little blown off a perturbed Annie responded, "I'm just worried that this guy is going to mess up many other women's lives before he's caught. If mobilizing the community is an effective means of tracking down this rapist, then I would think that the sooner we reached out to the neighborhoods of Olympia the sooner you would be able to get some solid leads to close this case. I also know that private citizens can do things that the police can't do because of a variety of legal prohibitions on what *you* can do."

"While that may be true, you shouldn't interfere in police business Ms. Lone."

"Well, anyway here's my number if you change your mind and want some help organizing the community. Thanks for taking the time to talk to me Detective Riley."

"Wilson…call me Wilson."

"Oh…um…thanks Wilson," stammered Annie before turning and walking toward the exit. As she walked toward the exit she wondered if he was watching her as she walked away. Looking over her shoulder, she saw Riley checking her out with a big smile on his face, which made her quickly look forward and pick up her pace toward the exit. Exiting the building, Annie swiftly crossed the street to get out of eyeshot of the detective without even opening her umbrella, getting soaked in the process.

As Annie walked down the sidewalk Rands walked up beside Riley and asked, "What did she want?"

"That's Annie Lone," replied Riley, still smiling. "She wanted to offer us assistance in catching the serial rapist."

"Maybe we could use her at some point in the future to get information out to the public. Or maybe misinformation out to the public with the hope of tripping up the rapist."

"I know but I didn't want to encourage her too much. Once we gather some real evidence we can use her."

As Rands began to summarize her follow-up on some witnesses she had interviewed, Riley's mind turned back to Annie. He had read every detail of her ordeal from the killing of Billy, her late husband, to her travails at Mount Baker Corrections Center for Women. He even watched the movie that had hit the big screen, watched all the news interviews she had done, and read her autobiography. The more he learned about her the more he liked her. She was smart, strong, and good looking. The very first time he saw her picture online he was taken with her. He thought she was the most beautiful woman he had ever seen. Here he had actually met her and couldn't quite believe his luck.

Riley thought he should ask her out but before he blurted out his desire to take her on a date his ethical compass kicked in and told him to pump the brakes before things got out of hand. He was on the clock and she was there to see him in his official capacity as a law enforcement officer. While some of his colleagues would take free coffee and other goods and services from the people they were paid to protect and serve as well as try to pick up women in violation of their police agencies' ethical prohibitions, Riley was not that kind of police officer. He wouldn't let his interest in Annie Lone get in the way of him performing his official duties and living up to the department's and his own high ethical standards. But damn, what a squandered opportunity, he thought, as his stomach ached at the missed opportunity that had presented itself to him. As his mind continued to wander, Rands broke his drifting minds spell by snapping her fingers.

"You listening to me, Riley?"

"Um…oh…yea…sorry, I just remembered something that I have to do tonight."

"It's ok. I was just summarizing the whole lot of nothing that I learned. So was she nice?"

"Who?"

"Annie Lone?"

"Oh yes. Quite nice and friendly."

"That's good for us. If we do need to get some kind of community action organized she will be a wonderful asset to put out in the field to get

Oly engaged."

"For sure! I guess we should probably talk to the Sergeant to make sure he's onboard with any plan to bring Annie Lone in to our case."

"Good point. Last thing we need is for someone to think that we are bringing civilians in without proper authorization from the chain of command."

"Yes we have to keep Internal Affairs off our backs," Riley said, handing Rands the piece of paper given to him by Annie Lone with her phone number on it before starting back toward the stairs with Rands closely following.

Irene arrived home at about 9 p.m. exhausted after putting all of her energy into trying to figure out who had kidnapped and raped at least five different women. She walked in, slammed her door, and tossed her keys on the coffee table. She still had to figure out what to eat for dinner but she was so tired all that she could do in this moment was flop down on the couch. She grabbed the remote control off of the coffee table and turned on the T.V.

Flipping through the channels, Irene searched for something to distract her from her gruesome job. She wanted to switch off her brain and not think about rape, molestation, or any other sexual abuse. The television landed on one of those classic romantic comedies. The point at which she started watching the movie, the two lovers were deeply engrossed in a montage of fun and romantic scenes. Irene was immediately absorbed into the movie.

The normally no-nonsense and often tough-as-nails Irene longed for a companion. A lover. A man to spend her evenings with. To go for walks on the local nature trails. It sucked that when it was time to unwind that she had to spend all her time alone. The first few years of living like this was fun but now it was monotonous. There was only so much space a gal needed to herself she thought.

Snapping back to reality after the romantic comedy went to

commercial, she realized that she had enormous hunger pangs. With that, Irene dragged herself off the couch and headed straight for her refrigerator to see what, if anything, she had that would slake her appetite and take her mind off of the loneliness.

CHAPTER 11

On her seventh week away from work after the kidnapping and sexual assault, Adrienne Niston, the twenty-two year old receptionist, sat in her room reliving her attack over and over again. Asking herself how this could have happened? How could she have let it happen? Wondering what had she done to draw this monster's attention? She couldn't summon the strength to face everyone. Hell she could barely face herself. Every time she used the bathroom she turned off the light so that she wouldn't have to look into the mirror. She felt that the person looking back was a stranger. She didn't know herself anymore.

Her sisters came to her mother's house week in and week out to check on her. They offered to take her on a shopping spree, asked her if she needed a ride to see her counselor, and put together picnic lunches. With all their might they tried to cheer her up, but nothing worked. She was in a dark place. Adrienne had always been prone to bouts of depression but the ball-capped monster's attack had destroyed all the progress that she had made over the last five years of counseling.

Even worse, she dwelled on what Jeffrey Motes would think. He was her fiancé; a tall dark and handsome man who had just graduated from the U.S. Naval Academy. He had been a superb student and cadet at Annapolis. They were set to be married next August in a ceremony on Orcas Island; a very beautiful place. A place chosen by Adrienne because as a child her parents took her there regularly and she had some of her happiest memories there. Native Northwesterners surely appreciated these little island gems in the Strait of Juan de Fuca and Adrienne was no different. However, all of her dreams were now on the line.

She had a positive pregnancy test result. The only way this was possible was from her rape. She had not even made love to Jeffrey, the love of her life, or any other man. She saved herself for him. The furthest they had ever gone was heavy making out and over-the-clothes contact but nothing else. They both restrained themselves from anything else because they anticipated a long marriage filled with wonderful love making sessions. As she sat in the dark, she started to cry for the hundred thousandth time. She cried because she knew she no longer had that gift to offer to Jeffrey. The gift of him being her first; the gift of having him be the father of her children. She had wanted this with him as long as she had known him. All she wanted was to be a wife and mother just as her own mother had been. She had no interest in career pursuits even though she had graduated from Auburn University with a Bachelor of Science in Chemical Engineering. She studied that subject because she was good at it and enjoyed it but not because she ever planned on working in the field.

Staring at the positive pregnancy test stick, Adrienne sobbed uncontrollably at what was lost. Her mother had told her that the U.S. Navy had given Jeffrey a temporary leave to come home and see her. He would be home within a day or two. How could she face him? He was supposed to be her first. This fucking animal had taken her against her will. He had polluted something that was intended for the love of her life. Her energy was simply depleted. All she wanted to do was sleep. She couldn't dare face Jeffrey after what had happened. It would be better if she was asleep when he got in. He would surely be angry. Why wouldn't he? She shouldn't have allowed this to take place. She picked up her prescription bottle without reading it and took most of the pills before climbing into bed to sleep. That's what she needed was a long sleep.

Adrienne adjusted her pillow to get more comfortable just as her eyes became extremely heavy with the periods of time between her opening them becoming longer and longer. Eventually, she couldn't open them any longer and finally surrendered. Adrienne started to dream. Her mind zeroed in on the first time she had met Jeffrey. They were both kids; just fifteen years old. Right out of the gate, Jeffrey tried to hold her hand at the mall. He was bold for a fifteen year old boy. She really liked him but was a bit nervous about holding a boy's hand. He asked her to the movies so often that she eventually gave in to his persistence. The movie he took her to was one of the scariest movies of the year. Just as he planned, he held her close when she jumped at the frightening scenes. As she remembered this happier time, even these thoughts faded with sleep overcoming her. Finally, there was nothing.

CHAPTER 12

Climbing onto a nearby garbage can, the ball-capped man found a loose screen on a small but high window into the garage. Using the large pocket knife he always carried he easily popped the screen out, slipped out of his jacket, held it against the window, and with one swift blow of his elbow broke the glass. Jackpot! Looking over his shoulder and seeing that no one saw him, his worries drifted away. The ball-capped man pulled himself through the window while standing on the garbage can as it rocked back and forth.

Once inside, he saw three empty parking spaces for cars and several rows of shelving units loaded to bear with all sorts of things. There were skis, snowshoes, ice axes, tents, large backpacks, and even two kayaks. Allison and her husband were definitely outdoor people. As he approached the door entering the house, he grew excited about the fact that he was finally going to get enough information about the beautiful Allison. Reaching for the door and turning the knob he was astonished to find that it wasn't even locked. Without any further hesitation, the ball-capped man entered the mud room and found a laundry basket filled with clothes just off to the side.

Initially ignoring its presence, he stopped when he noticed that there was a pair of bikini style panties poking from under a tee shirt. These were women's underwear. Allison's underwear. He slowly picked them up as if he had found some sacred relic that was too fragile to be handled carelessly. With them safely in his possession he took a long and deep whiff of them inhaling her essence. He could smell her. Womanhood! It was God's greatest gift to man; the one thing that made his life worth living after his mother's suicide. This trophy would hold him over until he was able to make her officially his.

With a sense of rising urgency, the ball-capped man stuffed the panties into his pocket, rushed from bathroom to bathroom frantically searching all of them on the house's first floor. Unable to find what he was looking for there, he quickly climbed the stairs toward the master bathroom. His watch showed that it was now 11:15 in the morning. He was not sure when Allison would be home but he didn't want to be there when she arrived. He wasn't ready for her. Everything had to be just right before they could be together. In an instant, he was rummaging through the master bathroom. He found exactly what he was looking for. It only took him an instant to make the switch.

With a big smile on his face, the ball-capped man made his way back to the garage where he climbed out just as easily as he had climbed in but before he left he took a few items out of the garage to make it look like a run-of-the-mill burglary if they discovered the broken window. Running wildly through the forest, he now knew for sure that he would have his woman. He would have Allison. She would surrender to his will. She would finally be the one to give him what he wanted. What he needed. All he had to do was wait for the right time to make his move. With sweat pouring down his face and still smiling, he charged forward through the marshy ground like nothing could slow him down. His goal was now within his reach.

Annie and Hannah Jane sat with a plethora of books splayed on the coffee table. Books they had gathered from the public library and purchased online from Congo shopping website. These books were all about serial killers and serial rapists and what makes them tick.

"The thing that I'm seeing common among these sex crime guys is that they all have some sort of 'God complex' that makes them feel entitled to do what they're doing," Annie said thumbing through pages of a book on her lap.

"Yeah, these guys are some real sick fucks," added Hannah Jane. "And they are a lot like those perverts who were running Mount Baker."

"True."

"This was a good idea. I don't know much about shit heads like these and I guess it makes sense that if we want to help catch them we have to know what kind of twisted fuck we're dealing with."

"We just want to gather enough information so that we can come up with a plan that will help the police put the cuffs on this rapist."

Sibyl walked through the front door with a fatigued look on her face.

"How was work girl?" asked Hannah Jane only looking up long enough to see that Sibyl looked like death warmed over.

"Uh. Tiring. I'm just glad to get home and get my ass into a bath," replied Sibyl laying her purse and keys on the coffee table after sliding her shoes off near the front door. "What are you two doing?"

"Research," Annie said.

"Yeah, we're trying to find out how to best help the police. So we're reading about serial criminals' proc….pro…cl," Hannah Jane tried to say.

"Proclivities," helped Annie.

"I'm sorry girls but I'm just too damned tired or I would help you go through those books," Sibyl said.

"No worries Sibyl. Go relax. We've got this," responded Annie.

"Thanks for being understanding," said Sibyl walking toward her bedroom unbuttoning her shirt.

Annie and Hannah Jane continued thumbing through the books and taking notes both hoping that their effort would pay off.

"Wilson, our second rape victim, Adrienne, is…dead. She took her own life yesterday," said Irene getting into the unmarked police cruiser's passenger seat with Riley.

"Fuck, Fuck, Fuck! She was just a kid. Just starting her life," shouted Riley pounding on the steering wheel. "We've got to go talk to her parents. I don't know what we can say but we've got to say something to them."

"Maybe we should go there first thing," said Rands her voice cracking.

As they pulled out of the police station's parking lot, Wilson was angry. He wanted to kill this rapist son-of-a-bitch. Riley had been in the Olympia Police Department's Sex Crimes Unit for a long time now but this stuff still got to him. He saw that as a sign that as long as he cared it meant that he would try his best to stop this shit from happening. The moment he stopped feeling anything he would retire and give up his badge because he would be useless to sex crime victims. He knew now that he had to step up his efforts to catch this animal. Even he felt that he, Rands, and the rest of the force weren't doing enough to stop this degenerate piece of shit. He would have to come up with some unconventional methods to put a stop to this animal's reign of terror.

Rands' eyes were filled with tears but she stifled the sobs that wanted to escape from her soul. She tried with all her might to contain her emotions but hearing the news and seeing Riley's reaction had caused her to remember something that she had long tried to forget from her own past. In college, her roommate and best friend, Lindsy, had been the victim of a sexual attack. The whole incident flooded back to her in that moment.

While attending Texas State University at the start of their freshman year, they had been invited to a party at one of the major fraternities on campus. They along with ten other girls from their floor of the dormitory walked to the party together. They were all excited and nervous. On their way to the party all of the girls had talked about watching out for one another if someone had had one too many drinks.

What a party it was. The beer was cold and plentiful, the music was live and loud, and the cute boys were abundant. Rands and her roomie started dancing with one another spilling beer from their cups on one another as they kept bumping against each other on the crowded dance floor. After a while the girls drifted apart chatting with various friends, doing shots, and eventually meeting up again in the bedroom of a guy named Stephen who had a wide array of drugs for them to sample.

Both girls sat on the end of his bed as he chuckled about something said by his buddy who sat in the corner holding a bong as if it were some sacred artifact.

"You girls want to try to some coke," Stephen said using a playing card to prepare the cocaine for snorting on a cutting board on a little table in front of his bean bag chair.

"Um…we've never done anything like that before," said the eighteen-year old Rands with an air of embarrassment, "I don't know."

"No worries. More for me," said an excited Stephen. "So what are you girls into?"

"We just wanted to come to this party to meet some new people and have a good time," answered Lindsy.

"Do you guys mind if some of my buddies come party with us?" Stephen asked after pulling a cell phone from his pocket and looking at it.

"No," replied Rands with a nervous excitement in the pit of her stomach.

"Not at all," Lindsy added with a big smile.

In that moment, five guys entered the room along with three additional girls all of whom appeared to be college aged. With that, Stephen began passing around the cocaine and his stoned buddy in the corner fired up his bong taking a few hits before passing it around the room to others. While Rands and Lindsy didn't do any lines of cocaine or take any bong hits, they drank plenty of beer and before they knew it were absolutely hammered. The girls that had joined the group soon wandered off under the influence of the cocaine. One could be seen through the cracked bedroom door on her knees voraciously sucking the cock of one of the guys that had come in with her, which made Rands feel a little embarrassed having never seen nor engaged in any kind of sexual activity herself. The other four guys as well as Stephen and bong boy both hung around the room.

Stephen started kissing the visibly drunk yet smiling Lindsy. She readily kissed him back while rocking back and forth. Rands sat next to Lindsy feeling a little awkward as Stephen began rubbing her breasts over the clothes and then unbuttoning her blouse. Lindsy didn't protest at all. In fact, she started to moan.

"Lindsy, we should probably head home now," Rands said.

"I'm okay. We're okay," Lindsy stammered.

"No I don't think so. I think we should probably head back to the dorm. We're pretty hammered."

"You heard what she said," chided Stephen.

In a matter of seconds, Lindsy's blouse was crumpled on the floor. Rands stood up and took Lindsy by the hand and pulled her but she pulled away from her.

"No! I want to stay here," yelled Lindsy.

One of the guys in the room, she wasn't sure who, pushed the stumbling Rands making her easily fall to the floor. Before she knew what happened one of the guys tore Rands' sweater off and fondled at her breasts.

"Dude, this chick is fat and freckly. Gross!" shouted the fondler.

"We've got Lindsy over here. Come on. Forget her," Stephen said.

Stephen laid the nearly unconscious Lindsy on the bed and reached under her skirt and removed her panties while all the other guys started pulling down their pants. Rands tried to get to her feet to stop what was about to happen but she was so drunk herself she had a hard time getting to her feet. When Stephen saw her trying to get up he walked over to her and grabbed her in a bear hug and held her as each guy climbed onto the now unconscious Lindsy and pumped away until each had an orgasm. What was clearly visible was Lindsy had never been with any man sexually and, even worse, none of them used a condom.

Once they were done using Lindsy and tossing another round of insults in Rands' direction for being fat, the cocaine-fueled college rapists simply left the room as if nothing had happened. It took Rands twenty minutes to gather herself enough to finally get Lindsy to some sort of semi-consciousness to get her downstairs and find some of their more sober dorm mates to help her carry Lindsy back to their room. Back at the dorm Rands called the campus police and reported the rape of Lindsy who by this time was even more conscious and completely unaware of what had happened to her.

The campus police, following university procedure, transported Lindsy and Rands to the local hospital. Where a rape kit and blood draw were done both of which later showed several different men's semen inside her and that Lindsy had been drugged by one of her attackers. While a rape kit was not performed on Rands, a blood draw was and it showed she had also been drugged but she didn't completely blackout the way Lindsy had the night of the rape. As it was later explained to them, the difference between the girls' sizes may have been a factor in why the petite Lindsy lost consciousness but not Rands.

The defense lawyers tried to get the boys off the hook for what they had done arguing that there was no evidence of who drugged Lindsy and that it wasn't his clients but after a long grueling trial anchored by Rands' testimony, because Lindsy had no recollection of the events, each of the rapists was convicted for the rape of Lindsy and sentenced to prison. Witnessing what she had and having to retell the story in front of a jury with the defense lawyer trying to dismantle what she remembered, took a heavy toll on Rands psyche. She had a difficult time maintaining relationships with men. The event had also steered her in the direction of becoming a law enforcement officer. She felt that she needed to do something with meaning in her life.

She and Lindsy had not talked to one another since the trial. Lindsy blamed Rands for what happened because she pressured her to come to the party that night and didn't get the animals off of her. Lindsy didn't remember Rands trying to extract her from the situation. She didn't remember anything at all. Lindsy eventually killed herself by jumping off an overpass in front of a big rig because of what happened to her, or as she told herself, what she had let happen. Now Rands sat in the passenger seat reliving those memories after Adrienne Niston's suicide. She would never forget that college experience. It would weigh on her like an anchor for the rest of her life. She was absolutely distraught with tears streaming down her face. With the death of Adrienne, it was as if she had failed yet another rape victim. The remainder of the ride to Adrienne's parents' home was in complete silence as her sadness and Riley's anger prevented either of them from being able to speak without an emotional explosion.

CHAPTER 13

Daryn sat at the kitchen table reading the newspaper with Julia devouring a bowl of cereal as Hannah Jane stood at the stove scrambling some eggs.

"Annie, looks like one of those poor girls that got raped killed herself. What a shame," said Daryn with a mouth full of food.

"Which one?" Annie queried.

"Says her name was Adrienne Niston."

"That guy needs his ball…I mean, needs to be caught," added Hannah Jane remembering that little Julia was sitting at the table. "What are we going to do about this Annie? We can't just sit on our butts."

"I know. I just haven't figured it out yet. And what do you mean we? You can't be a part of this. You're on parole supervision," replied Annie.

"So are you. It's not a violation to fight crime," Hannah Jane smirked.

"Alright, I'm still developing a plan for us. It's just taking me a little longer than I expected."

Hannah Jane switched off the stove element she was using and walked to the kitchen table and started putting generous amounts of eggs on everyone's plates. After emptying the remainder of the eggs from the skillet on her own plate, she placed it in the soapy water in the sink before opening the oven to remove a pile of nicely browned bacon and placing it in the middle of the table so that everyone could take as much as they wanted. Annie placed a strip in front of Julia who immediately went to work eating it.

"Well," said Hannah Jane before taking a big swig of coffee, "I'm sure that you can come up with something. This guy is no different than Draper and all the others we had to deal with at the prison."

With a fork in hand, Hannah Jane dove into her heaping pile of scrambled eggs. Sibyl came out of the bathroom and took her seat at the table.

"What are you guys talking about?" Sibyl asked.

"You don't want to know, honey," said Daryn from behind her newspaper.

"It's just more sad news related to the serial rapist here in town," added Annie.

"Oh, okay," Sibyl said taking several strips of bacon and putting them on her toast before piling eggs on top them and placing the other piece of toast on top of the eggs. With the wonderful looking breakfast concoction completed, Sibyl picked it up and took a big bite. With her mouth full she said, "That's *good*. Thanks for breakfast Hannah Jane."

"Oh yes, thank you so much Hannah Jane," jumped in Annie.

"No worries girls. It's a pleasure making breakfast for such a motley crew of broads," Hannah Jane said.

Annie had started putting together some ideas that might help the police draw out the rapist but they were far from being well thought out. She had to make sure that any plan she came up with wasn't something that would get her and Hannah Jane into any trouble because of their status after being released from prison and didn't endanger anymore women. Annie picked up the newspaper and stared at it for a moment before little Julia bound into her arms. Kissing her little nose Annie remembered why she fought so hard to get out of Mount Baker Corrections Center for Women.

Annie remembered that her number one priority in life was Julia and nothing or anyone else could ever supersede her position. This little girl deserved her mother's full attention, her love, and, most important, her presence. She also felt a pull in her heart to help others. Especially, to help other women in danger; during her travels around the world she encountered all manner of issues affecting women. Whether it was domestic violence and employment discrimination in Europe, the unpunished forcible rape of women in India, the mutilation of female genitalia in Africa, the suppression of women and girls based on so-called religious/cultural customs, or the termination of female fetuses in China, Annie felt her calling was to help her fellow woman.

Annie tore her mind away from these thoughts when the telephone began ringing. Sibyl answered it and handed it to Annie. It was her literary agent who wanted to talk to her about publishing an additional book. Annie listened as her agent droned on about the opportunity presented to her. Annie couldn't concentrate on what on what her agent was saying because an idea had popped into her head. She asked the agent if she could call her back then hung up the phone.

"Hannah Jane, let's go. There's something we need to do."

"Now?" Hannah Jane asked still eating.

"Yes, right now. Mom, can you watch Julia for me for a little while?"

"Of course dear," smiled Daryn.

"Thanks mom," said Annie kissing Daryn and then Julia. "I love you Julia."

Walking out the door with Hannah Jane carrying her plate and still eating, Annie thought long and hard about what questions she needed to ask.

CHAPTER 14

Riley and Rands got out of their unmarked car and quickly proceeded up the walkway past a well-manicured lawn and through a beautiful array of flower beds lining the path to the front door of the Niston family home. As Rands started to knock on the door, it swung open and there stood Adrienne's father, Peter Niston. He was somber-faced. His eyes were red with dark rings around them from a lack of sleep and crying since his daughter's death.

"Come on in detectives," said Peter. "I remember you two from the hospital. We saw you coming up the walkway."

"Thank you Mr. Niston. We just want to give you our condolences for your loss," Riley said. As the detectives entered the room they saw Annie and a woman they hadn't seen before sitting on a couch hugging Adrienne's mother, Christine Niston.

"Detectives, this is Annie Lone and her friend, Hannah Jane. They both stopped by to offer their support to our family. You know Annie Lone from that Mount Baker prison incident?" Peter asked.

"Yes. We know Ms. Lone," Detective Rands responded with a quick knowing glance to her partner, which Annie and Hannah Jane both noticed.

"Christine found Adrienne. She went to go wake her up for dinner but she was completely unresponsive," said Peter. "It's just so...so heartbreaking. She and Jeffrey had so many plans." Christine started to sob again hearing Peter talk about the lost future of Adrienne.

"I'm *so* sorry Mr. Niston," whispered Rands placing a hand on his shoulder.

"Mr. Niston, we would like to ask you a few questions as a part of our continued investigation. Are you up to it now or would you rather we come back later on?" asked Riley.

"Yeah. Let's do it now. Anything to put this animal away," Peter said with his voice cracking a little.

Looking at Annie and Hannah Jane, Riley asked, "Could we get some privacy because some of these questions are sensitive?"

"It's okay if they stay," Christine murmured. "They're here to help too."

"If you're okay with it then no problem. Did Adrienne receive any phone calls or mail from any strangers in the days leading up to her death?" asked Riley.

"No," replied Peter. "But she was reliving her rape over and over again. She talked about it with Christine. She tried to convince her to go see her counselor."

"So she was seeking counseling after her attack?"

"No, Adrienne has had a problem with depression since she was seventeen. She had been in counseling since then and it helped her significantly. The rape just set her back."

A crying Christine added, "All she wanted to talk about was what he did to her and how it wasn't right. How it ruined her and Jeffrey's plans. She felt that she had betrayed Jeffrey. She had been saving herself for him. I couldn't convince her not to think about it. I couldn't get her into the car to go see her counselor. I knew that it would help her if she just talked to her counselor."

As Christine talked, Jeffrey stood at the top of the staircase. He heard every word. His eyes filled with tears. He loved Adrienne. He loved her more than anything else. He had loved her ever since they met in high school. To him she was everything he ever wanted. She was silly, smart, beautiful, and, most important, she was his future. He couldn't have imagined life without her but now he would have to spend the rest of his days suffering through the loss. A flood of emotion rushed up inside him, which caused him to surge forth down the stairs where he blurted out, "She never betrayed me. I…I would never hold it against her what that son-of-a-bitch did to her. I love her. I wish I could have gotten home sooner. Maybe I could've done something to convince her. Telling her over the phone that I loved her wasn't enough. I needed to be here."

"Oh Jeffrey!" cried Christine getting up off the couch and grabbing Jeffrey into a strong embrace. "Deep down inside she knew that you loved her. This depression and the trauma had just consumed her. Don't blame yourself."

"Son, don't beat yourself up too much. It's not your fault," Peter added placing a hand on Jeffrey's shoulder as Christine held onto him tight.

"But I could've done something. I just feel so helpless. I don't know what to do," cried Jeffrey as he collapsed onto the couch holding his head in his hands sobbing. Christine and Peter both took positions on either side of Jeffrey trying to comfort him in the midst of his pain.

The entire scene reminded Riley of the first suicide he had to deal with in the aftermath of a rape. It deeply scarred him. He remembered the husband's wailing. Fearing for the life of the man, Riley visited him regularly for nearly six months. What he clearly remembered was that time brought about some healing but the husband never really got over it. The man told Riley that the thoughts of his wife crept into his mind at the least fitting times. He would be in the middle of lunch with friends and a song would come on that reminded him of her driving him to the brink of breaking down. He would excuse himself and go to the restroom to gather himself. Whenever he looked at their house he saw all of the projects that she wanted him to finish, which eventually forced him to sell the place. Riley knew all too well that Jeffrey faced this same ominous future. Love and sadness are not a good combination because they both team up to whip your ass like nothing else you've ever experienced.

"So her depression is what you believe caused her death, Mr. Niston?" asked Riley.

"No, it was the rapist. My daughter found out a few days ago that she was—sorry Jeffrey but she didn't want us to tell you because she wanted to tell you in person—pregnant," Peter said with tears streaming down both cheeks. "It was her first time. She couldn't bear the fact that it wasn't Jeffrey's baby."

Jeffrey began sobbing again. It stoked everyone else's emotions, which resulted in a flood of tears. A tear streamed down the normally stoic and professional Riley's cheek. His partner Rands glanced in his direction and worked hard to choke back her own emotional response to what they had just heard. Annie and Hannah Jane weren't so controlled joining Adrienne's family in their emotional outpouring.

"We obviously didn't want this in the paper you know to protect her memory," added Peter attempting to pull himself together.

"I understand," said Rands standing on her tiptoes to give Peter a hug.

"Mr. Niston, I promise you this. I won't stop until I put the cuffs on this guy," said Riley.

Everyone struggled to regain their composure after the strong outpouring of emotion. While there was a bit of embarrassment from them all, they at once understood that they were all in the same position. Feeling Jeffrey's pain. A pain that would haunt him for some time at the loss of Adrienne. But what was clear, he had a strong support group in Adrienne's parents.

"Thank you for your time. We'll get out of your hair and let you have your privacy in this tragic time," said Rands. With that Riley and Rands exited the house after receiving hugs from Jeffrey, Peter, and Christine along with an invitation to attend Adrienne's funeral service. They both had learned something that no one outside of Adrienne's family, her doctor, Annie, and Hannah Jane knew. The rapist had impregnated Adrienne. They now had the rapist genetic profile. Getting into the car, Riley and Rands minds turned from sadness and anger at the loss of Adrienne to a dogged determination to come up with the rapist's identity using this new evidence.

CHAPTER 15

As Annie drove away from the Niston's home, she felt that she finally had something to work with. Now it was time to stop this animal. But how?

"What are we going to do?" asked Hannah Jane.

"From the looks on the faces of those two detectives they didn't know that she was pregnant," responded Annie.

"What does that mean for how we're going to help catch him?"

"We've got to talk to some of the other victims to see if any of them are or were pregnant first."

"Right! Right! I understand we gonna catch this motherfucker now. Right?"

"Definitely, but we've got to draw him out. I think I know what we need to do on that front."

"I just felt like shit sitting there with them while they suffered. There was nothing we could do."

"I agree Hannah Jane. I felt helpless too."

Feeling a bit blue and uncomfortable in the wake of talking to Adrienne's family, Hannah Jane tried to change the subject.

"So you hot for that handsome piece of man chocolate, huh?"

"What...No...What? What makes you think that?"

"Well, I think he's for sure hot for you. I saw him cut his eyes your direction a few times and I think you're hot for him too. You want a slice of that man pie, Annie? Don't be embarrassed because so do I. You know it's been a while for me and I suspect it's been more than a while for you girl. There's only so much self-finger banging a gal can stand."

"Oh jeez Hannah Jane," Annie replied, turning red.

"I'm just saying a girl has needs and he's a great way of satisfying those needs. That smooth dark skin of his. Those damned arms of his are so big and strong. He must spend a lot of time in the gym to get them like that. I'm sure you would like to know what it feels like to be engulfed in his muscly embrace. Mm mm, while I've never been with a black guy before there is a first time for everything," said Hannah Jane wearing a devious smile.

"Gosh Hannah Jane, you sure have a one track mind. Anyway, I think he's a nice guy but that's it. Let's focus on catching this poor excuse for a man for the time being."

"Okay, if that's what you want. I'm just thinking we're human after all and one of the things we need as humans is sexual contact with other humans. Without it, we end up being old, unhappy spinsters. We can talk about this rapist if you want though. So what are you thinking?"

"Well, we've got to talk to the editorial board of the Olympia Herald."

"What about?"

"You'll see soon enough, Hannah Jane," responded Annie. She had decided there was only one way to go after a guy who hid in the shadows stalking his victims. However, Annie's thoughts did return to Riley. Yes, he was a very handsome fellow. But she wasn't sure if she had the time to commit to meeting someone and dating. She had all of her business and career ventures, speaking engagements all over the world, not to mention her top priority, Julia. How would she have any spare time to dedicate to a romantic relationship? At the same time, she had to admit to herself that it would be good to have an intimate companion. A person you could talk to about anything. A person to cuddle with on the couch and in bed that would give you comfort and a feeling of security. When she really thought about it, she missed sex. It had been a long time since a man had given her any pleasure.

In the last two years of her marriage with Billy, she didn't have much in the way of satisfaction. She missed feeling the touch of a man. Annie was relatively simple in her sexual desire too. Though she was a little apprehensive of exposing them to other people because of their awkward size, Annie loved having her feet massaged. If a man did a good job of that he more likely than not was going to get lucky. Realizing that her mind had drifted to a very naughty place at a time that she should be thinking about more serious matters, Annie focused on the road and on the matter at hand as they continued.

CHAPTER 16

The ball-capped man sat in front of his computer staring at the screen with tears streaming down his face. The computer had Adrienne's obituary on the screen along with her picture. How could she have done to this to him? What a selfish bitch he thought. By killing herself, she had killed his child. Their child; conceived in love. He didn't want to read the entire obituary but he had to. As he continued to plow through the sad text, he looked for it. His anticipation grew. As the obituary continued, there was no mention of it. Her fucking useless parent's didn't even acknowledge his child. The barbaric people hadn't even named the poor baby he thought. Reaching the end of it he realized that her family was a callous bunch of imbeciles without the dignity to recognize that his innocent baby had been murdered by her.

As his face grew red and scrunched with anger, the ball-capped man tossed the computer monitor to the floor. That wasn't the end of it either. He buried his foot in the drywall, which was followed by a rampage of raucously, deranged destruction. Everything from the coffee table to the two lamps in the room wound up feeling his *righteous* anger. As he sat on the floor huffing and puffing in the wake of his explosive outburst, he tried to gather his thoughts but it was so difficult to get them organized. He realized he needed to clear his mind. He needed to calm down. He was blinded with rage over his child's death.

This wasn't productive. This rage would make him vulnerable; vulnerable to making mistakes. Besides he could sire more children. He was going to sire more children. This wasn't the end. It was his high duty to sire children with these women. He'd already picked Allison Silson to be the mother of his next child. Yes, Adrienne betrayed him the same way his mother had. She had killed his child. But this time he would see to it that this next baby made it. He instantaneously knew that he had to keep Allison up to the last moment before she went into labor.

Growing calmer, he began to accept that he would have to change his approach. He would also have to make sure he didn't select anymore mentally ill women with which to have children. Trying to take his mind off of the tragedy that he had suffered with the loss of his child, the ball-capped man decided to go out and engage in a time-honored activity that often relaxed him. He would go scouting for future prospects. Pulling himself together, the ball-capped man got to his feet and surveyed the destructive consequences of his actions before he simply left the house.

Sitting in Best Drip Coffee, the ball-capped man, sans ball-cap, sat in a back corner pretending to read a novel and sip a cup of coffee. The coffee shop bustled with activity. There was a young couple sitting side-by-side at a table whispering in each other's ear with broad smiles on their faces. Directly in front of him, there was a middle-aged man pounding away at the keys of his computer. He had an intense look on his face as if he were putting together some super important report for work. Three men sat at a table discussing a business deal that they were negotiating while drinking coffee and eating pastries. The queue was extremely long with all manner of people standing in it. Some were dressed in shirts and ties. Others wore tee-shirts and shorts despite the usual Washington overcast skies and cool breeze blowing in from Budd Inlet. The baristas behind the counters were working extremely hard at preparing mochas, lattes, and cappuccinos.

The ball-capped man wasn't really paying much attention to any of that at all. His focus was trained on much more interesting things. He was intently listening too, and watching, the women who were in the coffee shop. He watched a red-headed woman wearing a sun dress who was probably about fifty pounds overweight in her mid-forties with large D cup breasts. She was talking to her husband on her cell phone. He paid close attention to her conversation for a while. She talked about what was going on at her office that day, what they were going to make for dinner that evening, and about attending some neighborhood barbeque on the weekend.

Next, a blonde twenty-something woman with an athletic build with size B breasts caught his attention. He watched her impatiently standing in the line waiting to place her order. She kept looking at her smartphone checking the time and for text messages with an annoyed look on her face. She wore yoga pants that showed off her very nice figure. She was very attractive even though she seemed to be in a very displeased disposition at the moment.

His attention was soon drawn away from her when a beautiful brunette exited the women's restroom wearing Capri pants and a tank top. She sauntered up to a burly man with dirty blonde hair and planted a huge kiss on his lips. The two immediately held hands and exited the coffee shop with the look of happiness on their faces. All of this activity really had the ball-capped man fired up. He was really aroused by all three of these women. He wanted them all but he knew that he could only choose one at a time. This was like a smorgasbord for him.

He still had to get his dear Allison first. When thoughts of Allison popped into his mind he felt warmth wash over him. He cared for her. He wanted her to be the mother of his children. She was the chosen one but who would be next? While he was deeply engulfed in thought the red-headed woman had looked at her watch and quickly left the coffee shop. At the spur of the moment, the ball-capped man rose to his feet and followed her out. He wanted to find out more about her. She was interesting. He had made his choice about who would be after Allison.

CHAPTER 17

"Thank you Ms. Bell for sharing that terrible experience with us," said Rands exiting Hilda's apartment with Riley in tow.

"Anything to help you catch him," replied Hilda clutching a tissue with both hands.

As Hilda closed her front door, the detectives walked toward their unmarked patrol car mulling over what they had just heard. Rands finished capturing the notes from the conversation in her investigation notebook standing next to the passenger door.

"Well, she's the last one. This confirms our suspicion that he had gotten them all pregnant," Rands said. The two get into the car and pull out of the apartment complex parking lot.

"Pretty sure we've got a rapist with a God-complex of some sort," said Riley.

"We've got to keep the fact that they all had abortions close to the vest. Who knows what this son-of-a-bitch will do if he finds out."

"But how's he able to time his attacks so that he gets them when they are ovulating?"

"Plain and simple," responded Riley. "He's fucking stalking these women beforehand. You want a coffee? It's on me. I'm just going to stop here at this 24/7 Slurp & Burp Mart."

"No," said Rands while Riley pulled into a parking spot and exited the car. She sat in the car and watched him enter the store, pour a cup of coffee, pay for it, and stop at the newspapers by the front door where he stood for a long time eventually picking up a paper and returning to the cashier where he paid for it. Opening the door of the car Riley tossed the newspaper onto Rands lap.

"Look," he said pointing to a sentence at the top of the page that read ANNIE LONE'S OP-ED.

"What the hell is this about?"

"I'm not sure but I'll drive while you read it."

Riley pulled the car out of the parking lot. Rands flipped through the pages and began reading the article.

"I meant read it aloud," declared Riley.

"Oops, sorry," Rands said. "Well, the title of the Opinion Editorial is 'Dear Ball-Capped Rapist.'" It read:

> What you have done to these women
> is reprehensible. Even more, it's barbaric.
> The belief that a man can take a woman's
> body because he chooses to is the worst
> of all crimes. It's more evil than murder
> for at least the murderer ends the victim's
> suffering. Instead, predators like you
> extend the suffering. You want the
> victim to live on remembering you and
> what you've done to them as if it were
> some dream come true. What's worse is
> that your actions led a person to kill
> herself rather than live with the remorse,
> shame, and anger of what you had done
> to her. This is truly the fruit of your
> poisonous logic.

So I am here to say to you today stop hiding in the shadows. Come out. If you believe what you're doing is somehow justified, why hide? Regardless, whether you emerge from the shadows or not, we will catch you. We will see to it that you get prosecuted, convicted, and imprisoned for the rest of your life you animal. When I say we, I don't mean the police. I mean my friends and all of the women of Thurston County. We will work overtime to catch you. Whatever your sick plans are we plan on stopping them.

Women of the South Sound: Start carrying weapons on you when you go out. Pocket knives, guns, mace, anything that you feel comfortable using against an attacker. You have the right to fight back. You have a right to your bodily integrity not being invaded by this monster. If at all possible, stay together in groups of two or more. In the meantime, be aware of your surroundings. Watch out for anyone who may be staring at you, following you, or any conduct that makes you feel uncomfortable. Let's work together to make it as difficult as possible for him to attack anymore women.

As you all know, there have been five women kidnapped and raped in Olympia. The Olympia Police are doing the best that they can but I say we as a community have a responsibility to work together to help cleanse our community

of this vile scourge. If you want to
discuss anything, please contact me at
(800) 555-1234. At a future date, we plan
on holding a forum for the women of
Thurston County to get information
about what's going on as it relates to the
serial rapist. Stay tuned. Thank you.

Folding the paper, Rands said, "She's sure stirred up a hornets nest."

"Damned right! She's probably compromised our investigation. This guy will do one of two things. He will either get scared and go into hiding for an extended period of time, which will make it nearly impossible for us to catch him or become angry and emboldened, which will cause him to go after some other poor lady to teach *her* a lesson."

"And he may well come after her now," added Rands.

"No doubt. We've got to get over there and ask her what the hell she's doing. She's endangering herself and everyone around her."

"You're really worried about her, huh?"
"What? No. Like I said she's putting herself in harm's way."

"Is that the only reason you want to go see her now?"

"What?"

"Riley, if I didn't know any better I would say you're hot on this chick," teased Rands.

"Yeah right! How'd you come up with that? I'm just trying to do my job and…"

"You don't have to explain yourself to me, Riley."

Pulling the car to the curb with a serious look on his face Riley said, "Get out!"

"Screw you Riley. I'm not getting out."

"Not so funny now," chuckled Riley. "I'm just yanking your chain Rands. Besides, why are you so concerned about my romantic interests? You should focus on finding some of your own."

"Hey buddy, I actually have an interested suitor, thank you very much."

"This is the first I've heard of this 'suitor.' What's his name?"

"Well, don't laugh but…I don't know."

"How do you know he's interested?" smirked Riley as he drove the car away from the curb.

"I go to the same lunch hangout every Saturday and I see him there and he sees me and always smiles."

"He's just being…"

"Shut up and let me finish…he has paid for lunch for me on numerous occasions."

"You had lunch with him?"

"No, when I went to pay for my lunch the cashier told me that it had been anonymously paid for by some guy. But I pressed her the last time and she told me it was this guy."

"So you have a secret admirer. I guess he's a shy guy. That's far more interesting than some supposed romantic interest between Annie and me."

"Whatever. I know you want her," chided Rands feeling a somewhat strong desire to get to know her anonymous lunch guy just as much of not more than Riley wanted to get know Annie.

"Let's not try to change the subject Rands. When was the last time you went on a date? I'm sure it was ages ago."

"Pay attention to where you're going. You just passed Annie's street."

Riley turned the car down the next block and headed to the roundabout to circle back. He was happy to hear that Rands had someone interested in her. While he gave her a hard time quite frequently, his best friend was a very kind woman who deserved someone special in her life.

As Riley and Rands came to a stop in front of Annie's house, they watched several people placing items into the trunk of a blue sedan.

"Annie, you better come out here," shouted Hannah Jane. "The fuzz just pulled up."

Annie exited the house holding Julia in her arms. Seeing the two detectives she immediately knew what they wanted to talk about and was prepared for a lecturing. She also felt a little nervous excitement about seeing Riley. She remembered the first time she saw him at the police station that she was quite turned on by his very presence. But they weren't there for that so she quickly focused her mind on the task at hand.

"So I take it you saw my op-ed piece?" asked Annie with a serious look on her face.

"Of course," grunted the annoyed Riley. "Why would you want to poke the bear like that?"

"Somebody's got to get that scumbag to come out of the shadows," Annie strongly retorted handing Julia to Daryn as she took the child back into the house.

"We know Annie but this may drive him underground, which means we'll never catch him," added Rands.

"Well, someone had to do something. The police department's silence is deafening. There hasn't been much communication in the media about what you're doing to catch this S.O.B. Women are really scared and I'm trying to bring him out. I want him to face the music. Knowing a narcissistic asshole like him, this will more likely than not bring him out," ranted Annie.

"What evidence do you have of this?" chided Riley.

"Well, the fact that he impregnated that poor girl Adrienne suggests some serious personality disorder or mental illness. Heck, this guy probably thinks he hasn't done anything wrong at all. He probably feels invincible and will be indignant at a woman who challenges him," Annie shot back.

"Yeah! And he's a piece of shit too," spat a fired up Hannah Jane.

"We just want you to let us do our job and not put yourself in danger Mrs. Lone," said Riley in a calming voice.

"Thanks for the concern but don't worry about us. We're big girls. We can take care of ourselves," Annie replied.

"By the way, what's going on here?" Riley asked looking around at the suitcases in the trunk and those that were still on the ground outside the car.

"Well, Detective Riley…" Annie.

"Call me Wilson," said Riley annoyed that every time they meet she continued to call him Detective Riley.

"Um…Wilson, sending everyone out of town for their own safety since this lunatic may come after me I don't want to endanger the people I care about. My mom, Julia, and Sibyl are all headed out of town."

"What about Hannah Jane?" asked Rands.

"Hey Occifer, don't worry about me. I can take care of myself. I'm staying here to help Annie if the degenerate does show up," smiled Hannah Jane.

"Did you just call me 'Occifer?' Oh, never mind. Detective Rands and I have a duty to keep the public safe and that even includes you so if you're doing something that's putting yourself at risk of attack by a dangerous suspect it's our job to talk you out of it," said Riley. "No matter how noble the cause."

"Man," said Hannah Jane. "I didn't know you felt that way about Annie. Want me and Detective Rands to give you two some privacy because…"

"That's not what I said," added Riley thoroughly embarrassed.

Annie's face turned a bright shade of red with Hannah Jane's uncensored comment. Riley's partner tapped him on the shoulder convincing him not to embarrass himself any further trying to explain. Trying to spare herself or Riley any further embarrassment, Annie said "I understand what you mean Wilson. It's just that…"

Hearing her call him Wilson caused a warm feeling to well up inside his chest, which immediately blocked out everything she was saying. His mind wandered. He thought that there might be a chance between the two of them. He was very attracted to her. He had become quite infatuated with Annie. His partner might have been joking but he really wanted to get to know Annie better. Realizing that he had drifted off into his thought, Riley snapped out of his trance and began listening to Annie who had continued talking.

"…We didn't want to interfere or make your job harder in any kind of way at all."

"I know Annie," Riley said. "We don't want anything to happen to you. And…and your family."

"Thank you for being concerned Wilson," said Annie hearing the concern in Riley's voice.

"Break it up love birds," joined Hannah Jane. "We've gotta finish getting these guys packed and on the road." Annie's cheeks turned a bright shade of red at Hannah Jane's remark.

"We'll get out of your hair then so you can finish," said a concerned Riley giving Hannah Jane a quick displeased glare while handing Annie yet another business card.

"I do believe this is the third time you've given me your card but I'll take it."

"Be safe ladies," said Rands.

"Take care Annie," Riley added.

After they got into their unmarked police cruiser, a smiling Rands whispered, "You're really into Annie?"

"Honestly? Yeah I am," said Riley as the car pulled away from curb. He was taken with her. It was everything about her. Of course she looked wonderful. But her feisty attitude and strong personality really added to her attractiveness.

CHAPTER 18

With the newspaper opened to the Editorial Page, the ball-capped man feverishly hunted-and-pecked away at the keyboard in front of him. Sweat beaded on his forehead but he did not remove the hat that covered his head. The ball-capped man had a fiery hatred in his heart for this…this…fucking Annie Lone. Who was this bitch to challenge him? Her name was vaguely familiar to him initially but when he looked on the internet he realized who she was. Why was she interfering in things that were no concern of hers? He needed to give her a clear message to stay clear of him or there would be consequences.

Women had a specific role to play in this world and he didn't want any liberal feminist mumbo jumbo being used to derail what he was doing. As the words flowed from his mind to the keyboard, he felt an outpouring of all that he had wanted to say to the world for so long. He knew that he couldn't just send this to Annie Lone. The whole world needed to know that what he was doing was justified. They needed to know that God wanted him to be the one to endow the world with his offspring. It was the right of every man under natural law. Without a break for eating or to use the bathroom, the ball-capped man worked on his statement to Annie and the world for why what he was doing was right. He plugged away at each key with precision and force as if his life depended on it.

Annie Lone and the others needed to be put in their place. They needed to know that man was the superior being of the homo sapien race. Women were intended for the purpose of satisfying man's sexual desires, producing offspring for man, and the mothering of those children. Women didn't have the same quick reflexes as men. They were physically weaker with lower bone density and less muscle mass. They let emotion cloud their ability to make objective decisions in the professional world. Most importantly, they needed men to protect them from the dangers posed by others because they couldn't do it for themselves. Because of all of this, he thought, they must accept their rightful position. How could they oppose the logic of it?

He vacillated on whether he should address the issue of forcibly impregnating women in his letter to the media. It was something that had to be openly advocated for but was now the time? He thought, they all really wanted *me* to get them pregnant. This point of view was based entirely on his experience to their reaction to his orgasm. So just from a purely mechanical point of view, the actions involved in sexual intercourse demonstrate this singular purpose. As an added bonus, nature made sex feel good to inspire humans and all other species to propagate themselves through procreation.

As he typed late into the night, the ball-capped man smirked because Annie Lone had motivated him. He knew that what he was doing was right. Society shouldn't be allowed to create maddening social rules that interfere with the laws of nature. With his forehead now covered in sweat, his smile widened as he continued to pound away at the keys on the computer putting together what he thought was the most beautiful exposition of his beliefs and the way the world should be.

CHAPTER 19

Walking through the door into the restaurant, Rands glanced around the room searching for the man who had secretly bought her lunch. Her eyes found him sitting at a table nestled in the back corner of the dining area clutching a cup and newspaper in either hand. She thought hard and fast about what to say to him. Simply saying "hi" couldn't be enough to break the ice. What about going up to him and just asking him out? She hadn't been on a date in a while and was a little unfamiliar with what to say. After wrestling with what to say she finally surrendered and decided to simply say thanks for lunch.

With her plan of action memorized, she started walking toward his table. As she approached the table, for the first time she saw him plain as day. He was absolutely stunning. His hair dark brown, his complexion was immaculate, and his eyes. Oh his eyes were a shade of blue that were warm and inviting like the Mediterranean around the Greek Isles that she'd seen online. She wanted to swim in those beautiful eyes. She started having second thoughts about approaching him. This damned guy was out of her league but before she could abort he spoke.

"Hi."

"Oh hi, I was just coming over to say thanks for lunch," Rands said nervously.

"You're welcome. Just thought a woman as pretty as you shouldn't be having lunch alone but I didn't want to come off as a stalker and invite myself to your table," smiled the man. "By the way, my name is Richard," extending a hand toward an already blushing Rands.

"I'm Irene."

"Do you want to join me?"

"I don't want to interrupt you reading your paper."

"Don't worry about that. Come on. Sit down with me."

"Sure, you don't mind?" smiled Rands as she took the seat directly across from Richard.

"Anytime I can have lunch with a pretty lady I never pass it up."

As their conversation continued, Rands was relieved that this guy was so easygoing. She was also excited to find out that he was truly interested in her.

She hadn't been on a date in so long that she didn't realize that this lunch had turned into just that, a date. She was happy that this guy was so warm and friendly. They talked about everything. She learned that his name was Richard Lock. He was a Fish and Wildlife Officer with the Department of Fish and Wildlife who had been with the agency for 13 years. Their conversation then turned to Richard asking Rands questions about her career and some of the craziest cases that she had seen in her time with the Olympia Police Department.

What was clear from anyone watching the two of them was that both Richard and Rands were interested in each other. They hit it off in a big way. They were both so absorbed in their conversation that neither of them paid attention to the time nor did Rands even bother to order any lunch to eat.

Finally, Rands thought, her long drought in the dating world was over. Maybe, just maybe, she would see an end to her lonely nights at home. A companion adds so much more to your life. Nearly everyone wants a person to watch television with, go for walks together, hold hands, and, of course, have sex with. She hoped Richard would be the right man for her. His outgoing nature and expression of interest in her surely gave her the impression that he was sincerely interested in her. As their conversation continued, both Rands and Richard wore broad smiles on their faces.

Hanging up the phone as Rands entered the room, Riley had an anxious look on his face. "About time you got back. Did you see Mr. Wonderful at lunch?"

"Yes I did and it was great. What's going on here?" asked Rands flopping down into her chair.

"All of the other rape victims have had abortions as well."

"We've really need a lead to stop this guy," said Rands sitting up erect in her seat upon hearing Riley's statement.

"It's absolutely atrocious what he's doing. We don't have much to go on either. No physical evidence, vague descriptions of him as a ball cap wearing white male, and a height ranging from about 5'11" to about 6'2"."

Rands tried to concentrate on the case but was unable to do so because her mind wandered to her lunch date with Richard. She hoped he would call her soon for another date. She wanted to talk to him more. She wanted to just hang out with Richard. It had been a while since her last romantic interest so she was a bit out of practice but she definitely wanted to get to know Richard. With butterflies still fluttering in her stomach, she decided to take a break from the case to go put some water on her face in the ladies room in an effort to calm the excitement from the impromptu lunch date.

"Sorry, Riley, I need to take a quick break. I'll be right back," said Rands as she walked off down the hallway.

Staring in the mirror, Rands told herself that she needed to get back into the game. Her hard shell had started to crack from this one lunch with Richard. She didn't realize how much she had been in need of companionship and how it had affected her. It felt wonderful having a guy interested in her. A handsome guy at that. However, this case was now her priority. Besides, she thought if they could work this case really hard and solve it she would have plenty of time to spend with Richard. Maybe she could even take some vacation days. After splashing her face several times with water, Rands grabbed a handful of paper towels and quickly dried her face. Pulling her thoughts together, Rands took another long look in the mirror, sighed, and marched out of the women's room.

Reaching her overflowing desk, Rands sat down and started rummaging through all of the documents. She saw that Riley was deeply concentrating on some large binder of documents open in front of him. Feeling frustrated, Rands stood up and marched over to the open door of Interview Room 3, now converted into a war room for strategizing to capture the ball-capped rapist. Rands combed over the evidence in an effort to make sure they had not missed some salient yet silent indication as to the identity of the attacker. With all of the evidence they had splayed out in Interview Room 3, Rands took a deep breath before going back to her desk.

"We've been through this too many times to count but there's nothing here," exclaimed an exasperated Rands.

"We know he used feminine hygiene products on the victims before turning them loose," grumbled Riley.

"Don't forget that there is evidence that he laundered the victims' clothing because one of them discovered a dryer sheet inside one of her pant legs after she was released…"

As Rands continued talking, Riley seriously considered the implications of this point. He mulled over an idea that popped into his head but believing it farfetched didn't want to mention it until he had some proof of the possibility.

Hannah Jane came out of the bathroom and looked at Annie. "What do you think?" she asked Annie.

"Wow! You look great."

"Stop pulling my leg. Let me go in here and clean this shit off."

"No. Don't. You *really* do look great. I've never seen you wearing makeup before but wow."

"Well, Thanks."

The forty-six year old Hannah Jane was a good looking woman and while her hard life had put more than a few wrinkles on her face she was still attractive. She hadn't been on a real date with a man in well over ten years. She had met a fifty-year old man named Willie while working at a local automotive repair shop.

"Well, tell me about this guy you met."

"Oh, he's just a guy who brought his car in for an oil change, to replace a burned out taillight, and to get a brake inspection. Kind of weird but oh well."

"What's wrong with that?"

"He came in three different days in the same week for these repairs. I guess he was mustering up the courage to ask me out."

"So he's really interested in you. Be careful Hannah Jane, you don't want to end up butt naked in his bed on the first date."

"Ha ha ha! You need to set up a date with that hunk of dark chocolate Wilson."

"Let's not get carried away. He's handsome and all but I don't have time to date right now."

"Suit yourself then but you don't want to end up an old dried up spinster with a bunch of damn cats do you?"

"Don't worry about me. I'll meet someone. So what time is he picking you up tonight?"

"Oh, he ain't coming here, girl. I don't tell guys I meet where I live. He could be a stalker or rapist or some shit."

"Good point."

"So speaking of the rapist what are we going to do about this motherfucker," she said while grabbing her car keys off the kitchen counter.

"I'm still mulling over what we need to do if he shows up but I have a few ideas bouncing around in my head."

"I was just wondering. Let me know when you get it all figured out cause I'm ready to catch another asshole. Right now I've got to get out of here before I'm late."

"Where are you guys going on this date?"

"He's taking me to the actor Rad Ditch's new movie at the mall."

"I want to see that movie too. It's supposed to be about a vampire apocalypse or something. Right?"

"Yes that's the one."

"Darn now I'm really jealous. Well, have a good time," said Annie hugging Hannah Jane tightly.

"Thanks," said Hannah Jane. As she closed the door behind her, Annie's mind turned to the ball-capped rapist once again. It had been a few days since she wrote her letter to the rapist in the local newspaper. She was anxious because perhaps Riley and Rands were right. Maybe her public admonition of the serial criminal forced him underground. Maybe the women who had been attacked by this animal would get no justice because he would pack his bags and disappear from the area. He would flee the state and go to another part of the country where he would begin his sexual assaults anew victimizing a whole new group of women and their families. Maybe she made a mistake. She wanted to draw him out. She wanted to get him angry and get him to make mistakes. His mistakes could lead to his arrest but thus far the rapist still hadn't responded to her taunt asking him to come out of the shadows.

She felt a twinge of guilt. Guilt that he would most certainly set up shop in a new town in a new state and resume his evil acts. These new victims would be all as a result of what she had one. It would be her fault. She felt like yelling because her idea was a failure. The rapist was going to destroy so many more lives now. She laid back on the couch with a feeling of despair haunting her.

Irene and Richard exited a high-end French eatery in Seattle and took a stroll through the city. They watched as seagulls floated about looking for any morsel they could claim as their own. The weather was its usual misty Northwest self. Irene's face wore a small contented smile. It was the first real date she had had in a long time and it was going well. She was absolutely giddy. Nervous butterflies still fluttered about in her stomach. She thought that being on the date would make it subside but it seemed to just linger. So much so that she couldn't even eat. She simply nibbled at a piece of bread on her plate and poked at her dinner entrée.

Richard spent most of the dinner asking her questions about her; her dreams and desires. While he answered every question she could get in about him, he always brought the conversation back to her. She could tell that he really wanted to get to know her.

"During dinner I couldn't help but notice your eyes. They are exquisite. Absolutely beautiful," Richard said.

"Thank you Richard."

"I wanted to tell you something earlier but I chickened out because I was worried you might not take it as a complement."

"Oh go ahead."

"Only that everything about you right down to those beautiful green eyes reminds me of my mother."

Irene awkwardly smiled at Richard as she said, "Sounds like a complement to me."

"Good. I was worried you'd think I was nuts for comparing you to my mother. Some women don't like being compared to a guy's mother you know."

"I know. But I understand that you're coming from a good place."

"Geez, I'm so glad you're okay with it. You resemble her so much. Eyes, hair color, height, facial structure…"

"Alright Richard. I get the point. Let's talk about you a little. What made you want to be law enforcement officer?"

"Well, mainly my stepfather, Harry Conne."

"Chief Conne's your stepfather?"

"Yep, not a lot of people know that he's my stepfather. He married my mom after my dad left us. He was good to her," said Richard as he stared out over Elliot Bay as the light of day faded and dusk overtook them. "He was good to me."

"So I guess you kept your biological father's name Lock?"

"Yeah, my mother thought that it was the right thing to do and Harry was ok with it also," explained Richard leaning against the fence.

"So you Fish and Wildlife Officers have the same arrest authority as we do. Right?" asked Rands.

"Yes we do. It makes it easy for us to deal with the varying types of situations that we happen upon while out and about."

"I understand that. Besides your stepfather, what led to you wanting to be a law enforcement officer?" Irene said as they continued walking.

"I really just wanted to help people. Not much else to it. I think that if each one of us takes up our responsibility to clean up society before you know it the whole damn world will be a better place to live."

"That is a very benevolent way of looking at things. My goal was simply to try to stop bad people from hurting others."

They continued walking and chatting for quite some time. All the while Irene was shocked at the ability of Richard to carry on a competent and interesting conversation. She hadn't met a guy this well put together in decades. It was amazing. It was more than amazing. Irene was elated. Her defenses came down when she was with Richard. She hadn't felt this secure with a man in a long time. Richard made her feel important; special even.

Looking at her watch Irene said, "I have to be up early tomorrow. We better head back."

"Sure," Richard said slyly placing one arm over Irene's shoulders. She moved closer to him signaling her approval as they reversed course heading back toward the restaurant where they had parked. "I would definitely like to see you again Irene."

"Ditto."

"I can't believe that as long as I have been in Oly I've never seen you."

The two enjoyed each other's company as they slowly walked back to the car in an effort to prolong the experience. The course of the date had Irene floating as she walked. This was the closest she had been to a man in years. It felt good. It was wonderful. Richard made her feel like a woman; a woman desired by a man. Not only was he handsome but he was really interested in *her*. While she was sure that he was certainly entertaining some sort of sexual attraction to her, she knew from talking to him that he wanted to really get to know her on a personal level.

Over the next two weeks, she and Richard would spend every free moment they had together. He treated her like a goddess. They talked about their future together. He even surprised her one weekend with a trip down to Seaside, Oregon. She had grown extremely fond of him. She felt the strong pull of love on her heartstrings. At first, she resisted but Richard was so kind, so sweet, and so caring that it was impossible to resist. He was the man that she had waited all these years to meet. He was the man that made her his number one priority in life. And his actions showed it. The man was so attentive to her. All that and he never once tried anything with her, which drove her to the point of having to immediately relieve the sexual tension after he would drop her off after their dates. While she was disappointed at his inaction, she understood that he wanted more but there's only so much a girl could take.

Tonight's last date ended like all of the others, he pulled her close to him and kissed her deeply. Kissed her like she was the only thing that mattered in this world. Like she was the very air that he needed to breath. After spending nearly ten minutes in his arms, they broke their embrace of one another and parted. Now, here she lay in bed after thoroughly releasing the tinderbox of sexual arousal that he had generated in her. She knew that she would likely have to be the first to make a move because he obviously had no current intention of trying to jump her bones. With that she turned over onto her left side, fluffed her pillow, and placed her head on it before falling asleep in breakneck speed.

CHAPTER 20

Hannah Jane's date with her former customer, Willie, was going well. The secret background check done by Detective Rands revealed that he had a DUI from twenty-eight years ago and a few bar fights when he was in the U.S. Marines but nothing since then. That news allowed her to let her guard down a bit. She decided to give him a chance.

She was trying to turn a new leaf. Stop falling for guys' lies. Start using her head. Stop using sex as a way to get what she wanted and as a communication technique. Start getting to know the man on a personal level beyond the size and girth of his penis. But she had to admit to herself she really did enjoy sex. Very much so. So this change would be extremely hard for her. However, Hannah Jane understood that she really needed to take her relationships with men to a deeper level. Now was the time.

Dinner went really well. The conversation was interesting. She thought at first that she was really interested in float planes because Willie thoroughly explained how flying them was different from other planes. But she really wasn't interested in float planes. She was, however, *into* Willie.

Now they were sitting in the theater waiting for the movie trailers to start. Willie seemed confident and relaxed. She had grown nervous at the thought of actually liking Willie and for a brief moment thought that it was too good to be true. He slyly lifted his left arm and placed it around her shoulders. Hannah Jane responded to it positively by relaxing her body against Willie's arm.

"I've been dying to see this movie," whispered Willie.

"Me too," responded a smiling Hannah Jane.

"I know it's fiction but the concept of discovering a lost human civilization from 25,000 years ago that had technologies unknown to modern history is so interesting."

"Fuck yeah it is. I saw a show on the Innovation Channel where they said that it's loosely based on some archaeological finds of cities that date back earlier than they originally thought we had cities. They also said that a comet may have hit earth wiping out everything about 13,000 years ago. I guess the collision led to a massive reset of human civilization because the previous technology was lost," Hannah Jane said confidently after spending several nights watching the show many times to avoid appearing clueless.

"Wow! You're pretty smart," Willie said.

"Thanks but I just love watching shows on the Innovation Channel. They always have interesting stuff on there."

"Well, we'll definitely have to get some pizza and get together to watch some of these shows."

"I'd love to do that."

The theater lights went down and the two turned their attention to the movie screen. Hannah Jane felt happiness like she'd never felt before. This guy was wonderful.

The Olympia Herald's Front Page read *Ball-Capped Rapist Emerges from the Shadows*. While munching on a piece of toast with peanut butter on it, Annie turned her attention to the article which included a letter from the rapist:

Dear Fellow Citizens,

Men and women are animals and have needs. For anyone to pretend otherwise is a farce. We as a species have an urge to engage in sexual acts. Women need to feel the strong touch of men. Men need to feel the soft pleasure of a woman's body. Because of this natural combination of the genders, we have procreation; the creation of a new being. To that end, I need to spread my seed. I have a right, as a man, to spread my seed to as many women as I want.

It is this natural order that leads me to believe that society has created arbitrary rules designed to inhibit us from doing what comes naturally. You don't see lions, chimpanzees, gorillas, polar bears, or any other male members of the animal kingdom restricting his desires based on the capricious concepts of monogamy or lack of consent. They take what they want when the want it. Hell, even in early human history a man could be a man. He could take as many women as he could successfully from his caveman brethren. He would provide them with security and food. They would provide him with what he desired.

Very few cultures or groups engage in this characteristically human practice anymore. For example, the Church of Latter Day Saints originally allowed men to take what was rightfully his but in a moment of weakness in the face of outside pressure the church abandoned the practice leaving its continuation to a small splinter group to preserve the tradition.

In our modern society, if a man wants a woman he has to beg and plead to have what she should surrender unto him. If he takes what should be his, then he is labeled a rapist, a sex offender, or a deviant. This is why I am advocating the repeal of all laws against raping adult females. Men of the world, you can thank me later for leading the revolt against these heinous restrictions on our rights.

As for those women who killed my babies, they will pay. You know who you are and don't think for one minute that I will be deterred in the slightest. I have already picked the mother of my next child and she will be ready for me soon. This time she won't have enough time kill my baby.

Annie fell back on her couch in disgust at the gall of this monster. Her stomach felt sick. She understood that the rapist was a vile piece of shit but this guy was inhuman. She knew now that she had to take drastic action to try to protect whomever the woman was he had already identified. She picked up her phone and dialed Riley's cell phone number. As the phone rang, ideas raced through her mind about how to stop this animal. None of them seemed at all possible or even legal.

"Riley here."

"Detective..."

"Call me Wilson," said Riley excitedly upon hearing Annie's voice.

"Sorry. Wilson, did you read the paper today?"

"Yes I saw his statement of intent, manifesto, or whatever he wants to call that drivel."

"We've got to do something now. He's already identified his next victim," yelled Annie in an exasperated voice.

"Calm down Annie! The Chief has already stepped up the frequency of neighborhood patrols and increased the number of officers on duty for the next forty-eight hours. There's not much else we can do at this point."

"Well, I've got a few ideas. I'm not sure if any of them will work though."

"Do you want to share them with me?"

"I...I better not. I don't want you to be involved in anything that may violate the suspect's rights or that may be unethical."

"Listen Annie. Why don't you come over, I'll make breakfast, and you can pitch your ideas to me. If they are too far afield of my job, then I will steer clear of any involvement whatsoever. If not, then I'll see what I can do to help you. What do you say?"

"I don't know."

"Oh come on Annie."

"Alright. But I don't want to be responsible for hurting your career in any way so if it's too crazy you've got to stay out of it. Okay?"

"Deal. My address is 1226 Pine Avenue in West Oly. You know how to get here?"

"Yep. See you in a few and I like cheese on my eggs." Hanging up the phone, Annie started searching for her car keys while mulling over what to do to catch this rapist. She had a large lump in her throat because she didn't know how long they had before the ball-capped attacker went after his next victim. Before leaving, she took a swig from her glass of water but it didn't help. The lump was still there.

"Annie those are all good ideas but they're all so dangerous," declared Riley forcefully as they sat next to each other on a couch with two plates with bits of scrambled egg on them.

"I'm no wilting violet or anything."

"I know but I don't want you to get hurt."

"I didn't know you cared so much Wilson," said Annie in a smart tone. However, seeing the look of concern on Riley's face, Annie felt a bit bad for making fun of his apprehensiveness. "Ok, I'll do my best to be careful. I promise."

"Good. I do…" said Riley before pausing realizing what was about to come out of his mouth.

"You 'do' what?" Annie asked anxiously.

"Forget about it."

"No don't forget about it. Tell me what you were going to say," chided Annie feeling the tension rise in her chest as her heart pounded. Riley didn't respond and Annie started poking him in his bulging bicep with her finger over and over again. "Tell me now. Come on spit it out."

"Stop Annie."

"Not until you tell me what you were going to say," she said continuing to poke him progressively getting harder with each poke. Without warning, Riley quickly grabbed Annie by the shoulders and pulled her in close to him so that their faces were within inches of each other.

"I do care about you. That's what I was going to say."

Looking into each other's eyes, they both converged on each other for a long heartfelt kiss. It was what they both had wanted. Annie simply melted into Riley's strong arms. In an instant, she felt safe; the safest she had felt since she had first met Billy. She knew that what was happening between her and Riley was for real. She could feel it. Now, she hadn't kissed a man in an extremely long time but she understood her feelings. While there was plenty of lust between the two of them, there was also true emotional attachment as well. She liked the fact that Riley worried about her. That he wanted to make her safe. She was attracted to that and at this moment it turned her on.

After what seemed like a half-hour of kissing but was really only about a minute and half, they broke the kiss and stared at each other.

"I…I'm sorry Annie."

"Don't be. I wanted that too," whispered Annie who looked down and saw that she had placed her hands onto Riley's chest and they were still there groping him. Even then she only removed her hands after caressing him a little longer.

"Wow."

"What?" asked Annie.

"Wow."

"What?"

"It's just that. It's just that you're a great kisser."

"Gee thanks. I thought I would be out of practice considering it's been a while since I last kissed a man."

"Seriously Annie I don't want you to put yourself in danger trying to go after this guy."

"I understand. But I've got to do something to bring this guy down before any more women are hurt by him."

With their conversation turning back to discussing how to catch the ball-capped rapist, the two of them eased out of the sexual tension that had grown between them during their brief but passionate encounter.

CHAPTER 21

Allison sauntered into the bedroom wearing an old-fashioned nurse's hat and a baby blue negligee that her husband, Harper, really loved seeing her in. She was nervously excited to let him touch her and for her to touch him. She worried about the fit of negligee because she had put on a little weight since she had last worn this little outfit. Getting to the gym was pretty hard with all of the housework and taking care of their toddler. Seeing the smile on his face when she walked into the room and the sheets raised like there was a tent pole under it, made her relax a little and get back into character.

"So you need the nurse to relieve the pain?" Allison asked in her best sultry voice.

"Yes I do. I have a lot of pain nurse," groaned a smiling Harper as he feigned being in pain.

"Where's the pain?" she said as she climbed up on to the bed and crawled over the top of him so that her body straddled his.

"Right here," said Harper pointing to his chest.

Allison leaned over him and began kissing his chest intensely. He rubbed her back gently as she continued to kiss each of his pecks. Then she slowly ran her tongue over his nipples making them hard little nubs. He felt an intense shock wave from her doing this that made him jump slightly.

"Where else do you have pain?"

Harper pointed to his stomach. "It's pretty painful here nurse. Can you relieve it?"

"Yes I can," replied Allison in a breathless voice before pulling back the sheets and pursing her lipstick covered lips and kissing him all over his stomach.

"Don't forget my neck nurse. It really hurts."

As Allison moved to kiss Harper's neck, he intercepted her lips with his own, kissing her deeply. Harper placed his hand between her legs and started softly and slowly stroking her making sure not to touch her clit. He wanted to make her excited and wet but didn't want to have her orgasm too soon.

Harper's efforts were so effective that she had to break the kiss and simply lay her head on his chest as the pleasure she was receiving washed over her. Allison began moving her body in an effort to make his hand touch her clit but he expended great effort to avoid touching it. She knew he wanted to make her orgasm using his mouth. She knew this because he always told her how much he loved to taste her and that making her feel good was his number one goal. Knowing this increased her desire to have him.

"I love you Allison."

"I love you too," she said wrapping her hand around the base of his stiff cock. But before she could do anything he had flipped her over onto her back and buried his face between her legs. As his oral ministrations grew more intense, she had both of her hands filled with clumps of his hair. At this point the tip of his tongue, playfully and vigorously fueled a flood of orgasmic energy throughout her body.

"Put your fingers inside me Harper," gasped Allison.

Obliging her request he buried two of his fingers inside her, which caused her to start bucking her hips toward his face in a feverish manner. Her movements were so strong that it made it hard for Harper to keep his tongue in contact with her swollen clit. Her grip on his head was like a vise as she lost control and squealed with joy from one of the strongest orgasms she had had in quite some time. After the orgasm had subsided, the two of them kissed for nearly five minutes sharing the wonderful fragrance and taste that had come from Allison.

Then Harper picked her up off of the bed and took her to just in front of the full-length mirror they had in the bedroom. Standing behind Allison, he slipped his cock into her. They stared into each other's eyes in the mirror as she moved slowly to meet his gentle thrusts into her.

"I love you Harper."

"I love you too sweetheart."

Harper continued to slowly move in and out of his lovely wife. She met each of his thrusts and even started rubbing her clit slowly while looking at her handsome husband and feeling the sexual desire grow inside her again.

"Harder baby!" huffed Allison.

As Harper picked up the pace of his thrusts, Allison's eyes had a fire in them. She wanted this man deep inside her and he wasn't moving fast enough.

"Harder!"

Harper grabbed her by the hips and proceeded to thrust into Allison with great speed and ferocity. Allison put her hand on the mirror to balance herself better as she arched her back so that Harper could go deeper.

"That's it baby. Give it to me just like that you gorgeous man."

"Oh Allison. You're gonna make me explode."

"Yeah! Are you ready to?"

"Yes, it's about to…" and before Harper could finish the sentence, Allison had pulled herself from Harper's tight grip, spun around, and thrown her legs into his arms thrusting her womanhood onto Harper's rigid cock with her back braced against the mirror. This caused him to have one of the most explosive orgasms he ever experienced as she proceeded to deeply kiss him while his body shuddered. Harper held Allison against the mirror tightly while he stood on weak knees trying to contemplate what had just happened.

"Wow! You've never done that before," stammered Harper. "How did you pull of such an acrobatic move?"

"I don't know what came over me," said Allison.

"I'm speechless right now," Harper said embracing her in his arms. "I love you so much. I couldn't imagine life without you."

The two just stood in front of the mirror holding each other. Both had satisfied smiles. More importantly, they both felt exceedingly close to one another.

Sitting high up in a Douglas fir behind Allison and Harper's home, the ball-capped man was angry as he stared at the two lovers through high-powered binoculars. He was furious. The fact that she was giving herself to this other man repulsed him. She was meant to be his. It was too soon for him to take her because the birth control would still be in her system at some low dosage levels, which would hinder their ability to conceive a child. With an air of disappointment engulfing him, he descended the tree in a cloud of fury. He needed to go blow off some steam.

As he gathered himself and trekked his way out of the greenbelt, the anger inside him grew exponentially as the images of Allison and that man kept flashing through his mind.

CHAPTER 22

"You want to come in for a nightcap?" Irene asked Richard with a wanting look on her face. She anticipated taking advantage of Richard. The best she had gotten out of him was several intense making out and heavy caressing sessions. Now she wanted more and had prepared for it including shaving her legs and trimming her untamed jungle that had been allowed to get out of control over the years. In her mind, there was no need for maintenance since there was no man in her life to break out the weed whacker for. Anticipating his response, "I even bought something special for you."

"Ohhhh!" smiled Richard.

"No. Nothing like that. I…I bought…some…bourbon since you said it was your favorite drink," laughed Rands.

"I'll come in for a nightcap anyway," chuckled Richard.

The two entered the one-story structure that was Irene's home. It was a quaint, well-organized place. With plenty of throw pillows on the couch and love seat as well as three ottomans for guests to prop up their feet.

"Have a seat," said Irene. "I'll take your coat."

As Richard handed her his coat he studied her place hoping to learn more about Irene's personality. She went into the kitchen and started pouring up some drinks for the two of them.

"Your place is nice Irene," said Richard flopping down on the couch.

"Thanks. It's not much but it's mine."

"I wouldn't say it's not much. It's really nice."

"Well, you're kind. It's the best a person can do on a police officer's salary," Rands said sitting down next to Richard and handing him a drink.

"Thank you," said Richard as he sipped his bourbon a couple of times before setting the drink on a coaster on the coffee table.

"I've really had a wonderful time with you over the past few weeks."

She worried about saying the wrong thing. She worried that she might scare Richard off if she overreacted in some way. Said too much. Said to little. She didn't know what to say. But what she did know was that the last words that she blurted out were a sincere expression of what she felt since meeting Richard. While she was definitely attracted to Richard, his personality, manners, and the way he treated her made feel something akin to love for him. She couldn't be sure if that was what it was but, damn, it sure felt like love. She didn't want to blurt out the words I LOVE YOU and make him head for the hills in the opposite direction but she felt she had to tell him something about the way he made her feel. The weeks they spent together and the fact that he was so kind and attentive to her needs…so sweet…this was something that every girl wanted in a guy. Here it was being served up on a platter. His attentiveness to her needs. The real fear that every woman has is that the feeling isn't mutual.

"Gosh, Irene, so have I. It's been amazing and…" before he could finish his sentence Irene laid a kiss on his lips. A kiss so unexpected that he was a bit caught off guard yet pleasantly surprised. Seeing the positive look on his face she smiled. With that Richard returned the kiss, which lasted much longer this time. In the midst of the amorous chaos, Irene started lifting Richard's shirt and rubbing his chest with both her hands. He broke the kiss to quickly rip his shirt off revealing a rather chiseled upper body, which made Rands melt while simultaneously apprehensive about removing her own shirt because she was a few dozen pounds overweight. However, throwing caution to the wind, she told herself to hell with it and ripped her shirt off too. This precipitated Richard pulling her close to him and re-engaging the kiss between the two of them and skillfully removing her bra causing her large breasts to bounce to freedom.

In an instant, Richard had effortlessly lifted her up on top of him and began sucking her nipples, which caused a pleasurable shockwave to overtake her. Barely able to hold up her own weight with her hands on the back of the couch and feeling that she was about to orgasm in a few minutes because of the level of sensitivity in her nipples Rands said, "Let's go to the bedroom."

"Okay."

Picking her up as if they were newlyweds, Richard looked into her eyes and asked, "Which way?"

Not saying a word, Irene pointed him in the right direction. She was speechless. She was going to be his tonight. His for the rest of their lives if he wanted. As Richard made his way to her bedroom she put her arms around his neck and rested her head on his chest. She still couldn't believe that this guy wanted her so badly.

He laid her on the bed and slowly removed her pants revealing her panties, which were covered with little hearts to his surprise. With a wide smile on his face, Richard said, "These are cute, Irene."

Before she could respond, he buried is head between her legs and began lapping at her cute panties with his tongue.

"You gonna take them off me?"

Without a word he pulled them to one side exposing her wetness where he immediately buried his face once more and in seconds she was on the verge of orgasm again because of the dexterous use of his tongue to bring her to the edge. In some magnificent way, he knew just how far to push her without letting her go all the way and she really wanted to. Irene groaned and thrust her hips toward Richard's face furiously as he caused her to feel like no other man had ever made her feel. When he finally allowed her orgasm, she lost complete control as it was the most intense she had ever felt. Letting out a yelp and grabbing Richard's head between her thighs, she bucked wildly to meet his tongue until she simply had no energy left.

Though exhausted, Irene was in heaven. Richard made her feel so special. So loved. That's right she thought to herself. She felt loved. Even more importantly, she definitely felt herself falling in love with him even more than she had before. Maybe it was the lust of the moment but whatever it was it felt real to her.

With Richard's head lying on her stomach, she felt extremely satisfied and a bit embarrassed that she had let go so much the first time; especially about the yelp. She generally was not a fan of performing oral sex on a guy but she was going to make an exception with Richard because he was so unselfish to her. Mustering up the energy to sit up on the edge of the bed and coaxing Richard to stand in front of her, Irene took Richard's erect manhood into her hands and looked him in the eyes and said, "Thank you so much." In one quick motion, she engulfed him in her mouth.

"You don't have to do that," Richard said as he lifted her face up and started kissing her again.

"No? But don't you want me to?" asked Irene.

"You don't have to do that unless you want to do it. Don't feel obligated though. What I did to you is because I wanted to do it. I've wanted to do that to you for a long time."

This made her feel even closer to him. She couldn't believe she had met a guy who would forgo the pleasure of a woman going down on him. This turned her on even more. It definitely made her want to do it to him.

"Yeah but you need..."

"Yes I do," said Richard grabbing his discarded pants from the floor and pulling a condom out of his pocket and tossing them back to the floor. "Would you do the honors sexy lady?"

"Of course," Rands said in her best sultry voice grabbing the condom out of his hand, tearing it from its wrapper, and quickly rolling it onto him. Before he could move, she had thrown him down on the bed and climbed on top of him and fully impaled herself on him. While she attacked his erection furiously bouncing up and down on it, Richard had returned to her breasts and this time he caressed them and tasted them slowly. He was in his element now. There was nothing better than being buried inside a woman while sucking her breasts. With her fully straddled over his body with his face buried in her huge breasts, Richard thought to himself this is the woman for me.

Irene was lost in a sea of pleasure. Pleasure fueled by strong emotion. The emotion of love. Love swelled in her because everything about this man made him perfect for her. For the rest of the night, the two lovers enjoyed each other several times.

CHAPTER 23

Rands walked into the office with an unusually happy gait in her step. She saw Riley leaning over a desk reading a document intensely.

"Did you find something?" Rands asked trying to switch from being a woman who just got some for the first time in a long time to a detective.

"Maybe," replied Riley in a low voice as he continued reading.

"Well, what?" Rands impatiently asked.

Closing the folder that laid in front of him, Riley stood up and said, "The autopsy confirmed that Adrienne Niston was pregnant."

"Okay?"

"The fetus is still in her body in the grave."

"And?"

"And it has her attacker's DNA in it. If we exhume the body, we'll have our first real evidence of who committed this rape," Riley said in a frustrated tone. "Looks like your date went well last night."

"Why do you say that?"

"For one, the last time you were off your game this much was when you had your date with Deputy Prosecuting Attorney Steve Wends. Not to mention that you have this 'I just had sex' glow about you."

"Whatever," Rands said turning a little red. "We'll have to convince her family that we need to exhume her remains to get a DNA sample."

"Yeah, I know. We should stop by and talk to them later today. The sooner we get her body exhumed the sooner we can find out who this fucker is."

"No doubt."

As Rands sat down and started reading some of the documents Riley had put on the table, they both sank deep into thought about the case and the fact they may have a big break after all.

"Mommy loves you Julia. Bye-bye," said Annie just before hanging up the telephone.

"How're they doing down there in Portland?" asked Hannah Jane as she walked out of the bathroom with a towel wrapped around her long hair and wearing a robe. The robe had been a gift from Sibyl. Sibyl had grown tired of seeing Hannah Jane walking around the house in a towel and having it frequently fall off exposing herself to everyone.

"They're okay. Just a little homesick but we can't take the chance of him coming after me and one of them getting hurt."

"Do you think he would really come after you? He's surely heard about the shit you pulled off at that damned prison. So he might be shitting his britches already because of that as well as the piece you wrote to the paper."

"These guys are usually arrogant chauvinists. I'm sure this one's no different than any of the others. The last thing they would think is to be afraid of a woman. That's why I'll be doing an interview in a few days to keep up the pressure on him."

"Damn girl. You sure are playing with fire trying to get that guy riled up," Hannah Jane said taking a seat on the love seat across from Annie.

"Well, I've got to do something to keep this guy from raping any more women. I think that the police have a limited amount of tactics that they can legally engage in but I, on the other hand, can do anything to draw this guy out so long as it's not criminal."

"Speaking of the police, what's going on with you and that hunk of man meat Wilson? You let that chocolate daddy spank you yet? I'd let him spank me any time he wanted. Hell, I'd let him do whatever he wanted."

Turning a little red with embarrassment Annie softly said, "No."

"You've got to give a horny single gal something to fantasize about while I play with myself."

"He's a good kisser."

"So you *have* kissed him…does he taste as good as he looks?"

"Alright that's all I'm giving you Hannah Jane," chuckled Annie.

"Come on. Does he have a brother or cousin? I'd settle for an uncle even."

As the two laughed, Annie's mind turned to the upcoming interview. She knew that it would likely inflame the rapist and cause him to come after her. She had talked to Hannah Jane about it and asked her if she wanted to go to Portland with Daryn, Julia, and Sibyl but Hannah Jane was a brave woman. Even more she was loyal to those who had shown loyalty to her.

Riley sat next to Christine Niston while Rands sat across from them wearing a somber look on her face in anticipation of the touchy subject that they were about to bring up. Peter Niston stood by the fireplace with a concerned look on his face having some idea about the subject of the conversation because when the detectives called they asked that both of Adrienne's parents be there. He was pretty sure that the rapist hadn't been captured yet because the media usually got those stories before even the family members of the victims.

"I wish we had better news for you but we haven't captured your daughter's rapist yet," started Riley.

"We figured that much detective," replied Christine.

"We're pretty sure there is hard evidence of the crime. In order to get it we have to exhume your daughter's body."

As the conversation continued, Peter and Christine's eyes filled with tears at the thought of disturbing their daughter's final resting place but they understood the necessity of what the detectives wanted to do.

"Yes," said Christine resolutely.

When it was all said and done, they wanted this criminal in prison. They wanted him to pay for what he had stolen from them and their daughter. It wouldn't be a happy moment but it would be a fulfilling one if it led to the capture of this rapist.

CHAPTER 24

Allison walked into the kitchen, opened the refrigerator, and took out her water bottle. After taking a long drink from it, Allison took a seat at the kitchen table feeling a little drowsy. She had worked out strenuously at the gym but not any more than normal. But maybe she had overexerted herself a little. She thought to herself maybe she needed to take a nap after taking a shower. As Allison stood up she collapsed but just before she hit the floor, a shadowy figure caught her and lowered her to the floor. She was completely unaware of his presence.

The ball-capped rapist's heart raced with anticipation. Here was his prize. The woman he wanted to bear his next child. He laid her limp body on the floor. Took the water bottle to the sink and washed it out thoroughly before returning it to the refrigerator. Once he was finished, he just stared at Allison. She was so beautiful; so vulnerable. She was about to be his, finally.

Realizing that he only had a limited window of opportunity, he picked her up from the floor and took her to the front foyer of the house where a large cardboard box lay open next to a handcart. Allison never noticed it because she came through the garage door. The ball-capped rapist put her into the reinforced cardboard box and sealed it. Placing the box onto the four-wheeled cart and making sure he had gathered up everything he had brought with him, the ball-capped rapist opened the door and wheeled the human cargo out the front door making sure it locked behind him.

As he reached the van he parked on the street in a manner that made it difficult to identify which house it was visiting, the ball-capped rapist carefully scanned the neighborhood observing two other service vans. While his was unmarked with any logo, it would probably not standout in suburban America. Once he loaded the box and the handcart into the van, he felt he had successfully pulled off yet another conquest. Starting the van, the ball-capped rapist released a great big sigh as he drove down the road.

Allison woke up a bit drowsy and confused as to where she was. She didn't recognize the place in the slightest but she did realize that her hands and feet had been restrained. She could also see that there was a whiteboard with what appeared pro-rape ranting written on it. In a flash, she understood that she had been kidnapped; no doubt by the serial rapist that terrorized women in the south Puget Sound area that the local media had been reporting on for the last several months. She immediately panicked. Fear had fully taken control of her as a huge lump filled her throat and sweat started pouring from her body. Who the fuck had done this to her? She tried to steady her emotions and control her thoughts. She tried not to think about who had done this or what he was planning to do to her. She tried to focus on not becoming a victim. While her heart raced, she implicitly realized that her best chance not to be a victim required that she not panic but stay focused on getting free.

Quickly getting her wits about her, Allison tried to sit up and survey the room for something that she could use to get free. It was difficult but she eventually was able to sit up by using an elbow on the ground to push herself upright. Her head pounded with a massive headache. She waited for the pounding to subside before doing anything else. When she tried to stand up, she nearly fell over because she hadn't realized that the restraints on her ankles were secured to the floor by a chain. Noticing that one of the four bolts securing the chain to the floor was loose, Allison began pulling the bolted chain back and forth with some urgency in an effort to loosen it from the floor, she hoped that the other three bolts would soon have some give in them.

As she frantically tugged at the chain, all she could think of was that she wasn't going to be a rape victim. Visions of her child and husband occupied her mind. She knew what was necessary. She had to resist. Hell, she had to fight. If this animal came in after her, she had to fight with every fiber of her being. Realizing that the four bolts were probably not going to loosen enough for her to get free, Allison's mind became preoccupied with finding other options. She hadn't seen the man who had taken her against her will. She knew nothing about how strong he was, how tall he was, or even if it was a single individual who had taken her. Being totally in the dark, her mind focused on devising some set of scenarios that she could use in nearly any case. She could kick him in his useless balls but he would probably be ready for that. Gouging his eyes would be nearly impossible with the way he had restrained her hands. This must mean that this guy knew exactly what he was doing.

Allison paused when she heard some heavy footsteps above her. She looked up a set of stairs toward a door but it didn't open. She knew that at any moment he could come in and attack her. As she listened to the noise upstairs she thought why her? Calming her emotions were much more difficult that she thought. She had tears streaming down her cheeks as she fought to control her fears. When did he do this? What was the last thing she had been doing? Then she remembered she was at home. She couldn't remember anything beyond that. He must've been in her home. He was waiting for her. No matter how hard she tried her last memory consisted of her walking into her house after coming home from the gym. After that her memory was blank. Having all of these thoughts allowed fear to creep into her mind again but she tried to use that fear against him and not let it work against her. She couldn't let it make her make mistakes.

"9-1-1, what's your emergency?" asked the operator.

"My wife, she's missing. I can't find her," shouted an exasperated Harper Silson as he held his son.

"Sir, how do you know she's missing?"

"Her keys, purse, and cell phone are all here at home as well as her car. I think something's happened to her. Please send someone," Harper pleaded.

"Sir, officers are on the way to your house. Are there any signs of an intruder?"

"No. I just got back from a birthday party with our son and saw her car in the garage so I assumed she was at home. She only went to the gym while we went to the party."

The doorbell rang and Harper went to open the door with two uniformed police officers standing outside. "There are two officers at the door," Harper told the operator.

"Okay sir. You can hang up with me and talk to the officers."

"Thanks," as the two officers entered the residence they looked around. Panicked, Harper started talking and made a strong effort to control his emotions as he spoke about Allison still holding tightly onto his son.

Hannah Jane was filled with anticipation and nervousness as she drove to her date. She liked this former customer of hers, Willie. She had grown fond of him after seeing him nearly every day for lunch since they met. He had also taken her out to dinner and to movies about a half dozen times. He was a nice guy. She definitely planned on following her friends' advice by not jumping into bed with him too soon. She wanted to make sure that there was a real connection between the two of them rather than relying on sexual desire.

She couldn't remember the last time she had butterflies in her stomach. What the hell? She wasn't a sixteen year old girl but she sure was acting like one. She'd spent hours with Willie. Why was date any different? Was it because they were going on the float plane tour over the Olympic Mountains in a tiny airplane where they would be in a tightly confined space? Was it because she wanted to kiss Willie and didn't want it to get out of hand by her giving in and having sex with him?

Pulling into the parking lot of the private marina, she saw Willie standing on a dock next to an aircraft. After parking her car, Hannah Jane took a deep breath before exiting the car. With her overnight bag flung over her right shoulder, Hannah Jane tamped down her nervousness and marched across the parking lot, down the ramp, and onto the dock where she was warmly greeted by Willie. He gave her a heartfelt embrace and a kiss on the cheek. This felt good. The nervousness she had was replaced by the feeling of happiness and excitement. Happiness to be close to Willie and excitement of getting to fly over the place where she had spent most of life and see it from a different point of view.

With the float plane gaining speed across the water, Willie talked to Hannah Jane to distract her and make her more comfortable since it was her first time. She laughed as he rattled off ridiculous jokes and told her stories about his wild and crazy fans. Settling into their altitude, Hannah Jane removed her headset and planted a big kiss square on Willie's lips. Smiling widely, Willie started pointing out interesting landmarks to her.

CHAPTER 25

Sitting in the movie theater during an early afternoon matinee with her head resting on Wilson's muscular shoulder, Annie felt, simply put, happy. Her eyes were fixed on the movie screen but her mind was elsewhere. She was in a state of bliss. She hadn't felt this comfortable and safe in years. Riley's presence, smell, and strength gave her a sense of joy and happiness. The heavenly place her mind occupied was disturbed by a buzzing sound. Riley quickly reached into his pocket and pulled out his cell phone. Annie's head came off of Wilson's shoulder.

"Hello," whispered Riley.

"We got another potential kidnapping," said Rands. "It's at 2312 Rolling Hills Circle. It's a thirty-five year old wife and mother. Her husband is distraught. I'm on my way over there now."

Before hanging up the phone, Riley put a hand over the receiver and said, "Sorry Annie, I've got to cut our date short. Duty calls."

"It's okay," Annie said.

"See you there in a minute, Rands," Riley responded as he rose to his feet, squeezed out of the row, walked up the aisle, and exited the theater followed by Annie.

"Annie, there's been another kidnapping. Come on, I'll drop you off at home," Riley said as he walked quickly toward the exit.

"Who's the victim?" asked Annie as the two of them exited the building into the parking lot.

"I don't know. I just know it's in Rolling Hills Estate."

"What's the plan?"

"Well, Adrienne's body should be getting exhumed at this very hour so in a matter of a few days, maybe sooner, we're going to know who our rapist is," as they both climbed into their seats and put on their seat belts.

"That's good news but what about the current victim?"

"We don't know if she's been taken by him or not yet."

"But I think you're pretty sure of it at this point."

"The best chance she's got is for us to get this guy's genetic profile from the fetus. We'll know either his name, if he's already in the system, or his DNA profile."

Riley hurriedly drove out of the parking lot with thoughts racing through his mind. First and foremost was the missing woman. He worried about her wellbeing. Hopefully, she can hold on long enough for them to find her. He worried about her family and how they would handle what had possibly happened to her. Riley's car sped toward its destination with a purpose.

The backhoe began digging into the fresh grave of Adrienne Niston. With a van parked nearby, Assistant Medical Examiner Susan Thorns stood by waiting for the casket to be loaded. After receiving an anonymous tip, a Seattle news crew was nearby filming and occasionally asking Susan questions. But Susan directed them to ask their questions to Olympia Police Department's Public Information Officer. Susan knew that her role was integral in tracking down the serial rapist. She already had a reputation as an extremely competent medical examiner. Susan often put an egregious amount of pressure on herself to do an effective job. This was the biggest case she had worked on in her entire career. As her anxiety grew she squeezed tighter and tighter on the coffee cup in her hand until it started pouring all over her glove. As the backhoe dumped one final bucket of soil, a worker attached some cables to the casket before jumping into the seat of a mini-crane and lifting the casket out of its tomb.

The mini-crane operator placed the casket about eight feet behind the van she was going to use to transport the casket back to the medical examiner's office. After shutting off the mini-crane, the worker and the operator of the backhoe joined Susan by the casket. Susan jumped into the driver seat of the van and backed it up so that it was closer for the two men to put the casket inside.

"Ready?" asked the backhoe operator.

"Yep," replied the worker who drove the mini-crane.

In unison, the two men lifted the casket and slid it into the back of the van.

"Thanks guys," Susan yelled from the open window of the van after the backhoe operator closed and pounded on the van's backdoor. She slowly drove the van off the grass of the cemetery and down the narrow windy cemetery road anticipating getting back to the office to get the ball rolling in the hope of finding out who was responsible for all of the attacks.

Harper and Allison Silson's home was filled with crime scene investigators. In the family room, a distraught Harper sat on the couch holding his son with one uniformed police officer standing nearby while Rands interviewed him. The crime scene investigators combed over every inch of the home taking fingerprints from doorknobs and window sills, taking photos, and looking for various other undiscovered evidence.

Riley parked his car out front and rushed in past four crime scene investigators on the lawn.

"Sorry I'm late," Riley said to Rands walking into the family room and taking a seat next to Rands. "Where are we?"

"I'm just finishing up my interview of Mr. Silson," replied Rands. "Mr. Sil…"

"Detective Rands, you need to see this," said crime scene investigator Don Johns.

"Excuse me Mr. Silson. We'll be right back," said Rands standing up and following Don Johns and Riley. The three of them entered the garage. Once inside, Don Johns stopped at the back of the garage in front of some metal shelves.

"Here," pointed Don Johns at a broken window in the corner adjacent to the metal shelves. "This is where he came in."

"How in the hell did he fit through that window!" exclaimed Rands.

"I know. The son-of-a-bitch must be a spider. That window can't be any more that 2 by 3 feet," Don Johns added. "We didn't get any fingerprints off this window. We collected the broken glass to take back to analyze though."

"So we know we're dealing with a slippery son-of-a-bitch," Riley said moving closer to the window to examine it.

The ball-capped man stood staring at the television in disbelief. On the screen, the news van was parked at the cemetery where Adrienne Niston was buried. Without even listening to the reporter, he knew he was in trouble. They had exhumed Adrienne's remains. This sent his mind racing in a panic. The only reason they would be disturbing her grave would be because they believed there was some evidence. Instinctively, he knew exactly what they wanted. His DNA from the fetus. He took off his ball-cap and immediately put the padlock back onto the door leading into the basement. He couldn't let them figure out who he was. If they did he would have to spend the rest of his life in a fucking cage; prison was his biggest fear. He wouldn't be able to handle that shit. Right away he knew that he had to take action to destroy any thing they might find that could get him a one way ticket to his worst nightmare.

Adrienne Niston's nude, reopened body was positioned on an autopsy table in the cold examination room. Susan stood over the tiny, barely recognizable fetus which was placed on another table. She worked meticulously to gather tissue samples for DNA testing. Working on the fetus was a rather disturbing experience for her. While she had worked with many dead bodies including children, she had never worked on a fetus. It caused her more than a little consternation collecting tissue samples from the fetus.

Generally, Susan was a rather unemotional clinician. Others in her profession found her unusually cold at times. However, she was nearly overcome with a feeling of sadness; sadness that this baby never had a chance. What affected her the most was the fact that she couldn't have babies of her own. A childhood illness had ruined her chances. Here she was at forty-two and married to a wonderful man who would be a spectacular father but they would never have the opportunity at the natural gift of making and birthing their own children.

Wearing a somber look on her face, she placed the tissue samples in sterile packets to be sent off for testing as if she was re-burying the baby. After placing the sterile packets in a shipping container with dry ice, Susan's shoulders relaxed because the worst part of what she needed was over. All was left was to hand deliver the tissue samples to the Washington State Patrol Crime Lab. Adrienne could be returned to her resting place and, hopefully, not disturbed again.

CHAPTER 26

Frustratingly laying the tablet on the coffee table with the screen still on the article about Annie's interview with the newspaper, Riley said, "Annie, why would you do this?"

"I didn't know you cared," Annie joked touching Riley's cheeks in an effort to console him.

"I'm serious. This guy could really hurt you. I don't know what I would do if…"

"Calm down there chief," said Hannah Jane walking into the family room from the kitchen. "We put our big girl panties on for this one. We ain't scared of no punk ass creeper."

"Stay out of this Hannah Jane. Annie's put herself in danger unnecessarily," exclaimed Riley.

"I'm just trying to help y'all out," Hannah Jane said walking back into the kitchen. "Besides, what about me? Am I just chopped liver?"

"Wilson, don't worry. We've got a plan if he shows up here. I know you care about me. I like that but I also have to do something to stop him," said Annie putting her arms around his waist and lying her head on Riley's chest.

"It's just that…that…I," before he could finish his words Annie pulled Wilson's face to hers and gave him a long, lingering kiss.

"I know Wilson. I feel the same way," whispered Annie taking hold of his hand.

"What you said in that interview will make him violently angry. You're basically challenging his manhood. While I don't disagree with what you said, I know he's going to probably come to try to 'teach you a lesson' if he gets the chance."

The both of them continued holding hands as they plopped themselves in the middle of the couch.

"We fully anticipated that reaction from him, which is why we'll be waiting for him when he shows up," Annie said.

"I can't be here as much as I want to but…"

"Don't worry about us. We've got it under control. Hannah Jane is my right-hand woman. If he comes in here, he's in for a rude awakening."

"I don't think he's going to come in here guns blazing the way you expect. From what we know, he stalks his victims watching their every move before striking."

"We certainly hope he does that. Anyway, enough talk about that asshole. Let's watch a movie or something because after tonight you're going to have to make yourself scarce around here. We don't want you scaring him off."

With a backpack flung over his shoulder, the ball-capped man dressed in dark blue jeans, a dark shirt, and gloves approached the back door of the medical examiner's office and used a crowbar to pop the door open. He thought to himself that this was his lucky day because of how easy it was to get into the building. The ease of it all made his pounding heart slow just a bit.

Even though he had surveyed the parking lot and seen that only the official vehicles of the medical examiner's office were there, he still wanted to tread lightly so as not to disturb someone who might be burning the midnight oil. The ball-capped man moved down the corridor past a triumvirate of offices on either side of him. At the end of the corridor he came to an alcove with a receptionist counter behind glass. He could see off to the left a room marked as MORGUE. It had a combination lock on it. He had not anticipated this hiccup.

Using the crowbar that he had popped the backdoor open with, the ball-capped man forced the locked door open. With a feeling of relief, he entered the morgue and started reading the labels on the freezers used for storing the bodies. None of them had Adrienne's name on them. They had a bunch of numbers instead. He didn't have time to search every single freezer compartment. Frustrated, he looked around the room thinking hard about what he needed to do next. Seeing a file cabinet through a window in a little office at the far end of the morgue, the ball-capped man quickly moved toward it. If he could find her file, it would surely show which numbered compartment her body was in.

Once in the office, he discovered that the file cabinet was locked. He could get it open but it would take a while using the crowbar because of the unusual locking mechanism used to secure the file cabinet. He would nearly have to dismantle the file cabinet to get at its contents. He thought to himself that since he had come this far he may as well finish the job. As he began to pry at the file cabinet's locks with the crowbar, he heard a noise. After listening to the noise for a moment and deciding that it was nothing, he returned to attempting to open the cabinet.

"Back up is en route to your location," said a female radio voice.

Upon hearing that, the ball-capped man was convinced that he was not alone. He quickly turned off the light in the little office and ducked just below the window taking occasional peeks out the door. What he didn't know was that upon forcing the door open, he'd set off a silent alarm. He finally saw a tall, thin Olympia Police officer enter the room with his gun drawn. The ball-capped man's heart began pounding at the sight of the officer. The first thought he had was that he was fucked. How was he going to get out of this? There was nowhere for him to hide. He didn't have a gun he could use to escape.

The responding officer easily surveyed the huge open space of the morgue and saw that there wasn't anyone there. Seeing the dark office on the other side of the morgue the officer slowly approached the room with his weapon aimed at the door. When the officer was within three feet of the door, he took a long hard look through the glass window just to the left of the door and looked around as much of the dark room as he could. With his attention focused on the door again, the officer figured that it was a little too far ajar in an unusual manner. Using his right foot, the officer kicked the door open, which caused it to bounce off the wall behind it and start closing in his direction.

"Police! Show me your hands now," commanded the officer but nothing happened.

The officer thought for a minute that maybe he should kick the door harder. Readying himself for a strong and forceful kick, the officer, with his firearm still trained on the door lurched forward with a great amount of force to kick the door in hopes of dazing the hidden burglar. As his foot made contact with the door, the officer felt an excruciating pain as the crowbar crashed down onto his shin. So much pain that he was blinded for a second and within that second the burglar that he sought had come out with a ski mask pulled down over his face wearing a ball-cap. The ball-capped figure quickly struck the officer's hand knocking the firearm from it and, in a flash, was out the door.

Lying on the ground in extreme pain the officer reached for his radio.

"Officer down! Officer down! The suspect hit me with something," he shouted into the radio.

"Your back up should be there now," responded the dispatcher. "Where's your attacker?"

"I think he's left already."

"Sit tight. I'm sending an ambulance."

Once outside, the ball-capped man saw several police cruisers in the parking lot. There was also an officer on foot who made eye contact with him. The ball-capped man immediately took off running toward a wooded area.

"Stop! Police," shouted the officer who chased after the ski mask/ball-cap wearing figure. "I'm pursuing the suspect north into the woods behind the medical examiner's office."

The other officers joined the chase as the darkly dressed figure went into the woods. Even though he was dressed in dark attire the officer who initially saw him stayed hot on his trail.

"Stop now," huffed the officer in a full sprint chasing the ball-capped suspect through the trees and shrubs. "Show me your hands, dammit."

The ball-capped man knew that he had to shake this officer if he had a chance. The last thing he wanted was for them to catch him because he would end up in a prison shit box. Fear of that scenario pushed him forward at full speed even though he knew these adrenaline junky motherfuckers wouldn't stop their relentless pursuit of him. He heard the officer pursuing him directing the others using his radio so they weren't far behind as evidenced by the light from their flashlights moving quickly toward him. With the officer close, the ball-capped man changed direction toward Andrews' Bog.

If he had any chance at all, it would be the bog that would give it to him. It would slow down the officers who were hot on his trail. Most importantly, it would also make it hard for the police dogs to track him and he knew that it would only be a matter of time before they arrived. As his heart raced at the thought of being caught, he knew he wouldn't be able to handle being caged like an animal, which motivated him like nothing before.

"Riley, sorry to bother you so late but we're at the medical examiner's office where there has been a break-in and we found a stolen van parked on a nearby street with a few clipped newspaper articles about Adrienne Niston's disappearance and suicide," said Detective Al Jones of the OPD Property Crimes Unit and an old police academy friend of Riley's.

"Thanks Al. I'm headed over there right now," grunted Riley sleepily.

"You should also know that we've got about thirty officers from our agency, the county, and state patrol pursuing a suspect through the woods right now. Last I heard he was headed toward Andrews Bog."

"This guy's smart. He knows that the dogs will be hot on his trail soon so he wants to throw them off. This is definitely our guy," Riley said as he nearly fell over trying to put his legs into his jeans in his mostly dark bedroom.

"Alright, we'll see you soon Riley."

"Don't let this motherfucker get away."

"For sure. We're throwing everything at him that we have."

Rands jumped into the front passenger seat of Riley's car still buttoning up her shirt.

"So the son of a bitch broke into the medical examiner's office. Pretty safe to assume that he knew we exhumed Adrienne's body," said Rands.

"Yep and he's worried. To go to that extent to try to stop us from getting the DNA of the fetus means he knows we're going to get him," responded Riley as he sped off toward medical examiner's office.

"I got a call yesterday early in the evening from the ME...Susan I think was her name. She told me that she had finished gathering tissue samples from the fetus and gotten them to the lab for analysis of the DNA."

"Once we get the genetic profile we'll be able to run it in the national and state databases," added Riley.

"I have hunch that we might not find anything so I might also run it in some other databases like the military."

"Good idea, Rands."

As the car pulled into the parking lot at the medical examiner's office, it was filled with vehicles including ATVs from the Thurston County Sheriff's Department and the Olympia Police Department, Crime Scene Investigators' vans, and the Washington State Patrol cruisers. Parking the car near the main entrance of the office, Riley and Rands quickly got out of the car and rushed into the building.

"Hi guys! I'm Susan Thorns," she said reaching to shake hands with Riley and Rands.

"Anything missing from here?" asked Riley.

"Nope. Detective Jones told me it was probably the serial rapist you two are trying the catch. The good news is that I've already returned her body to the funeral home for reburial and the tissue samples are safe in the lab. I took them there personally."

"Thanks Susan," said Riley.

"He did try to break into our secured file cabinet but the locks on that thing are nearly impenetrable. It does contain a file about what I did with Adrienne's body but that's it."

"Riley," shouted Detective Jones, "I just finished talking to the officer who first arrived on the scene."

"Where's he?" Rands asked.

"He's in an ambulance on his way to the hospital now. I asked him if he got a good look at the guy and he said the guy had on all dark clothes and wore a black ski mask with a ball cap on," Detective Jones responded.

"The suspect is headed into Andrews Bog. He just slid down a steep embankment about thirty feet. I think he might be hurt," an officer's voice called out over the radio. "There are six of us directly on his trail. We're leaving a flashlight on a tree for the K-9 officer to show her where we're going down to get this guy. We can hear the dog in the distance. Over."

"This is the OPD Watch Commander. Careful guys. You've got more backup coming with some off road vehicles," said another voice over the radio.

The three detectives rushed out of the office to join the pursuit of the suspect. Riley's adrenaline was pumping at an all-time high rate as he anticipated putting cuffs on the son of a bitch.

The ball-capped man had cut his leg on a small tree stump when he took a free fall down the steep hill side into the soggy ground of Andrews' Bog. His desire not to be caught helped him overcome the immense amount of pain he felt in his leg. Prison was not a place for a person like him. He wasn't a fucking animal. He didn't want to be locked in a cage. He wouldn't survive there long. He intended to remain free even if it cost him his life. Then he remembered Allison. Allison still locked in his basement needed him. She needed him so much. He needed her. She was going to bear him his first child. This time he would keep her for a few months to ensure that the baby would make it past the point at which an abortion could be performed.

Feeling no pain, he rose to his feet. At the top of the steep hill were five flashlights slowly making their way down into the bog. He knew that he couldn't stay still any longer. He took off sloshing through the muddy water as it soaked his shoes and slowed him to what felt like a crawl. If it slowed him down this much in regular athletic shoes, he knew that the officers pursuing him would be nearly paralyzed in the muck of the bog with their heavy boots. Emboldened by the circumstances, he marched onward toward his eventual destination on the other side. If he made it there, the law enforcement officers chasing him didn't stand a chance of catching him. With muck coming half way up to his shin, he soldiered on even as he heard the faint barking of dogs and what he thought was some noisy motor headed in his direction.

CHAPTER 27

Exhausted after hours of struggling to get free from her restraints, Allison finally relented to the fact that she was trapped. She slumped against the wall in defeat. From what she remembered from the news reports about the suspect, he raped his victims until they were pregnant. She understood that he was not going to kill her. But what he had in store for her...well, as far as she was concerned you might as well be murdered. He wanted to take her against her will. No one had ever done that to her before. Sure, she had the same experience many women had with a guy who became a little too hands-on but that was a regular part of the dating scene. Usually when a lady drew a line, even the skuzziest guy wouldn't cross it. This...this, what did the paper call him, ball-capped rapist...he wanted to force her to have his baby.

With a renewed will to resist, Allison carefully plotted, in her mind, the next steps. She couldn't get free from the restraints that held her chained to the floor but she could use them to her advantage. They may be the key to her freedom. She knew that her plan would require plenty of energy and since she hadn't eaten in a while the next best thing for her would be to rest. Maybe even take a nap.

"The suspect is somewhere in Andrews' Bog," said the lead officer pursuing the ball-capped man as he huffed and puffed exhausted from the extended chase.

"I have a hunch he's headed toward the Sound," shouted Riley into the radio furiously driving a noisy ATV in the direction of the officer with Rands on the back holding on for dear life. "We'll radio for our guys to get the OPD Marine Unit in the area to try and intercept him."

The ball-capped man was near collapse. He spent nearly all of his energy crossing the soggy ground of Andrews' Bog at a frenetic pace. Despite being fatigued he saw the light at the end of the tunnel. Budd Inlet was only a few dozen yards away. While the flashlights of the officers chasing him had gotten a little closer to him, Andrews' Bog had had its desired effect. It slowed his pursuers down to a near crawl. The anxiety about possibly being captured had begun to subside. Now he would have to ensure his escape and he knew exactly what he needed to do. Huffing and puffing with his shoes filled with cold, wet mud, the ball-capped man continued ahead as if driven by an instinctual desire for freedom.

"How the fuck did he go down this steep a drop off without killing himself?" asked Riley.

"This guy's got some serious motivation. He knows that if we catch him and charge him with these rapes he'll never see the light of day again," Detective Jones quipped.

"Actually, the son of a bitch fell down the hill, got up, and kept on going," replied the officer assigned to stand watch at the top of the hill to show the other law enforcement officers which way to go. "Then he just got up and kept on going as if it was nothing."

"This is the Oly PD Marine 1. We've arrived at the north side of Andrews' Bog," said an officer over the radio.

"Have you spotted the suspect?" Rands queried on the handheld radio she'd just pulled out of her pocket.

"Negative. There's no sign of the suspect," the officer said over the radio.

"Please be careful out there. He assaulted an officer at the Medical Examiner's office," Rands continued.

"We've got another unit expected to be onsite in about five minutes and…"

The radio fell silent.

"Marine 1? Come in Marine 1," said Rands as a shiver overtook her. "We've lost Marine 1."

"Anybody know a route around this damned bog?" yelled Riley.

"I do detective," shouted the officer.

"Take Detective Jones' ATV there," said Riley pointing at the blue machine. "We'll pick you up when we come back through."

"I don't mind riding on the back," added Detective Jones.

"Alright guys. Saddle up!" Riley said starting the noisy ATV with Rands seated behind him.

Marine 1 floated with its engine set to idle as the two officers shone bright searchlights out into the bog looking for any movement; any unnatural object that didn't belong to the landscape. The only thing the two officers saw was swamp grass, water, and mud. One officer talked on his radio, peered off into the bog, and operated a searchlight. The other officer used the remaining searchlight. The noise from the motor was loud enough to disguise the sound of the water as the ball-capped man climbed into the back of the boat. In one quick movement, the uninvited guest had taken the boat out of neutral and jerked to the left in one sudden motion causing the two officers to fall into the water. Before they realized what happened, the Olympia Police Department's Marine 1 was headed into deeper waters with the two officers floating and the ball-capped rapist at the controls.

The ball-capped man knew he was home free now. He would drop the boat off in an isolated area of Budd Inlet to make sure no one saw him abandoning it. He switched off all the lights on board of the vessel as he cruised along letting the wind flow through his hair. He usually would never been seen without his ball cap but it had to go. Once he entered the water, it had become saturated. The ball-capped man knew it was dangerous to operate a boat with no lights at night but he had to make sure no one could follow him.

Tromping out into the wet bog the detectives ran into the two OPD Marine Officers who had been dumped into the water. The initial officers to pursue the ball-capped man had already reached the two OPD Marine Officers who, by now, were thoroughly humiliated. Not to mention frozen from being in the chilly waters of the Puget Sound.

"What happened out there guys?" a perturbed Riley asked.

"He…he got the drop on us," one of the embarrassed officers responded with his teeth chattering.

"This was our best opportunity to capture this son of a bitch," added Rands.

"I can't believe the gall of this guy. Stealing a police boat? He's got a set of balls on him like a fucking elephant," a frustrated Riley said.

The entire group turned around and headed for the ATVs and made their way back to the Medical Examiner's Office consumed by a feeling of failure. The possible serial rapist was within their grasp and he had escaped. Detective Jones called to let the K-9 Unit know the suspect had escaped and to head back.

"Good morning Detective. It's Susan from the ME's Office. Sorry for calling you so early," said Assistant Medical Examiner Susan Thorns tightly holding the unopened envelope in her right hand.

"What time is it?" Riley asked in a groggy voice.

"Um, its 8 a.m."

"I guess I better get up and head into the office," said Riley rolling over onto his back and staring up at the ceiling.

"Um, I was calling to let you know the DNA profile is back on Adrienne's...um...baby."

"Okay. I'll stop by your office first thing. See you in ten minutes Susan," Riley said excitedly as he hopped out of bed and started gathering clothes in a hurried fashion.

"Oh. Alright. I..."Susan said but before she could finish her sentence Riley had hung up the phone as he put on two socks that didn't match. Realizing the mistake he dug through a pile of clothes laying on a chair next to his bed searching for matching socks. Riley had a hard time finding matching socks or anything else because his mind focused almost exclusively on this case. After last night's near miss at catching the rapist, he was ready to get his hands on the first real evidence they had in the case. Finally dressed, Riley quickly darted out the door toward his car anticipating putting the cuffs on the rapist bastard in a matter of days.

CHAPTER 28

The ball-capped man stepped out of the bath and began toweling off in earnest. He thanked his lucky stars after the previous night's intense chase through Andrews Bog. He'd only gotten about five hours of sleep but had to get up and prepare for a romantic day with his beloved Allison. He had anticipated it for so long and didn't want to ruin it by thinking of negative thoughts. He slipped into a pair of white athletic shorts and a blue tee shirt. After vigorously brushing his teeth and shaving, he unlocked the door to the basement to go in for his first sexual encounter with Allison.

As he proceeded to walk down the stairs his heart pounded. His hands were sweating profusely. He was nervous. Every time he was a nervous wreck as if it was his first time with a woman. Nearing the bottom of the stairs, he could see her beautiful face as she lay on her side fast asleep. He gently nudged her shoulder to wake her. Her eyes opened and all she could see was a tall figure wearing a ball-cap that was pulled down so far over his face that his eyes and the upper portion of his face was in a shadow.

Once Allison had fully awakened he used a key to free her from the restraint that kept her chained to the floor but didn't remove the ankle restraints.

"What are you going to do to me?" asked a worried Allison.

He ignored her question. Seeing the nervous look on Allison's face he rubbed her back in a soothing manner to calm her as he helped her to her feet.

"Where are we going?" she asked.

There was still no response from the ball-capped man. At the far end of the basement, there was a grungy looking couch resting against the wall. The ball-capped man guided her to the couch. He guided Allison to her knees on the couch with her facing the wall. He pushed her into a bent over position.

"Please don't take me this way. I know you're in charge. But please don't," Allison pleaded with her captor. "I'll do anything you want if you just don't take me this way. It really hurts when I do it that way."

Hearing the sincerity in her voice, the ball-capped man hesitated. She sensed his wavering and thought fast and furiously about how to capitalize on his moment of pause.

"If I didn't have these shackles on my ankles I could let you take me missionary. That's my favorite position. I promise to get my legs open as wide as I can for you and up as high as I can."

The ball-capped man retrieved a key from his pocket and removed the restraints from her ankles.

"Thank you. Please take my pants off now," Allison said.

The man quickly removed Allison's pants and underwear in two fast motions. She laid on the couch only wearing her shirt. He could see her neatly trimmed pubic area. He also saw the blue dolphin tattoo she had just above her pubic area off to the left. He reached to touch it but hesitated.

"Go ahead. It's okay. Just don't hurt me," said Allison.

He touched it and felt himself go rigid almost instantly. As he caressed her tattoo, he thought how fortunate it was that she wasn't resisting the way the others had. He was consumed with anticipation at the opportunity to have her. The front of his shorts had started to become saturated as he became more aroused. Seeing the dampness of his white shorts, Allison knew she had him.

"Shouldn't we get this party started," she asked.

The ball-capped man stood up and removed his shorts revealing his erection. Allison was mortified at how skinny it was. While it was long, it was not much physical substance to it. Its appearance made it look awkward.

He spat into his palm and gave it a couple of quick strokes. Then he moved to mount Allison but before he got the chance she kicked him in the balls with a force of a punter kicking a football to the other team. He nearly collapsed to the ground but his anger at being tricked gave a shot of adrenaline that overpowered the pain of the kick.

"You fucking bitch! When I'm done with you, you'll not be able to walk for weeks. I'm going to fuck your ass until it bleeds," the angered ball-capped rapist shouted.

He lunged for Allison but she kicked him in the chest with an equally dizzying blow before she delivered several vicious blows to his neck and head that caused him to see stars.

"Bitch!" shouted the rapist, struggling to draw in a breath, before jumping on top of Allison but she locked her legs around his neck just as he dove at her. What he didn't know about Allison was that she was a black belt in Taekwondo and was a blue belt in Jujitsu. She was glad to see her training pay off. With the man's neck clutched between her legs, she bore down with all of her strength on his neck. She could see he was turning red. He swung wildly at her face with his fists in an effort to get her to let go but her face was just out of his reach and the blows he was able to land were glancing and had only a superficial effect.

Allison knew she couldn't let the man go so she worked with all her might at cutting off the oxygen to his brain. As she squeezed his neck with her powerful thigh muscles, she felt his body slowly losing some of its strength. His face contorted and turned purple. She applied so much pressure that the ball-cap he wore on his head fell to the floor. Now, for the first time, she could see the man's face clearly. But it was so contorted under the pressure of her legs that it was hardly recognizable as a face. Her will to survive the attempted assault on her empowered her in ways she never thought possible. Her goal was to get back home with her family at all costs even if it killed the motherfucker.

With no letup in the pressure she applied to his neck, the ball-capped man collapsed. He was totally unconscious from the pressure she applied to cutoff the blood flow to his brain. The full weight of his body overcame her exhausted legs and the man fell on top of her in a violent crash as her legs gave way. She laid there absolutely spent. All the energy she had went into incapacitating this monster before he raped her. Now she didn't even have the strength to push this disgusting piece of shit off of her. Initially, she started to panic at the thought of not being able to move the much larger man off of her. Tears welled up in her eyes as she imagined him coming to and beating her senseless for what had been done to him.

Allison told herself that she needed to fight. She couldn't forget about her family; her son and husband. They needed her. She had to get out of here. Digging deep down for the strength, Allison started pushing at the limp body of her kidnapper. Allison cried uncontrollably at the thought of being there when he woke up. His weight too much to lift Allison started sliding her body out from under the passed out pervert. Finally freeing herself, Allison sat for a minute to catch her breath before reaching for her nearby pants. As she did, she fell to the floor because her legs were still not fully recovered from the fight with the ball-capped man.

She had been severely weakened by the battle. Despite this weakness, Allison put on her pants and got to her feet. She wanted to get as far away from this motherfucker as possible. She wouldn't be able to survive another fight with the man. She knew that she had only cutoff the oxygen supply to his brain via the carotid artery, she knew the man was not dead. He had only passed out and would eventually regain consciousness.

Her first steps were very weak. She could barely walk but sheer determination fortified her weak legs. Pushing through the exhaustion, Allison forged ahead. The more she tried the easier it became; especially at the sight of the passed out man on the couch. With the fear of the man waking and stopping her gnawing at her, Allison hobbled toward the stairs at breakneck speed and started climbing them. The more she thought about how much worse her predicament could be the more she pushed on toward her ultimate goal of freedom.

At the top of the stairs, Allison opened the door and locked it behind her. She wanted to do everything in her power to slow him down if he pursued her. Without wasting any time, Allison fled out the front door into the dissipating daylight. Feeling free as a bird she began to run through the forest. Not knowing where she was didn't hinder her in any way whatsoever. What mattered most to her was the fact that she hadn't been raped. What mattered even more was she would live to see her little boy and husband again.

CHAPTER 29

"Fuck! Fuck! Fuck! I can't believe that there's not one hit in the entire DNA database," a frustrated Riley said.

"I know. We were so close to getting him," added Rands. "It just means that this sick fuck has always been really careful. What next?"

"Well, we could search some unconventional databases. You know like the military and others to see if anything comes up."

"Good idea. But I think we need a federal court order to get access to the military records."

The phone on Riley's desk rang. Riley was thoroughly disappointed at the roadblock they had just hit in their case and was in no mood to talk to anyone.

"You gonna get that?" asked Rands.

With that Riley picked up the receiver, "Detective Riley here."

Just as soon as he had answered the phone he hung it up.

"We've got to get down to the hospital. Allison Silson was just brought into the ER," said Riley. They both grabbed their jackets and coffee cups before rushing out the door.

"I'll get a uniformed officer down there to stand guard until we arrive," responded Rands.

Parking their car outside the ER entrance in a parking spot designated for police, Riley and Rands rushed inside. They both walked briskly toward the reception counter and the security guard sitting behind the bullet proof glass pushed a button that unlocked the door from the ER lobby to the ER treating area. The nurse at the treating station recognized the two detectives and pointed them in the direction of Exam Room 5. Riley nodded at her before continuing on toward the room.

Pushing the door to Exam Room 5 open, Riley recognized the voice coming from the room. Once inside his suspicion was confirmed. Annie had come to the hospital. She was accompanied by her sidekick Hannah Jane.

"Annie, what the hell are you doing here? This is a criminal matter for the police," chided Rands.

"We came down to check on Allison," Annie responded. "We didn't see any officer."

"How the…" Rands started.

"They used a police scanner," jumped in Riley. "Annie, I've asked you not to interfere in police investigations. You've got to stop this."

"We only came down here to make sure Allison was okay because we were worried about her," Annie said.

"Detective, it's okay. These ladies have been so nice to me. Besides, I've always wanted to meet Annie Lone. I just wish it was under better circumstances," Allison jokingly said with her spirits a bit up after the earlier ordeal she faced trying to escape.

There was a knock at the door and a police officer poked his head inside the room. "Is this Allison Silson's room?" asked the young officer.

"Yep. Good job guy," Riley sarcastically said.

"Thanks Detective," said the oblivious young officer with a smile on his face.

"Okay, Annie and Hannah Jane we need you two to step outside so we can talk to Mrs. Silson," demanded Rands.

"No problem," Annie acquiesced. "Thank you Allison for talking to us."

Annie hugged Allison followed by the not-to-cuddly Hannah Jane hugging Allison as well.

Riley thought that Annie was complying with Rands request a little too easily so he asked, "Have you guys already talked to Mrs. Silson?"

Not saying a single word, Annie and Hannah Jane exited the room.

"Sorry about that Mrs. Silson. Those two are not authorized to investigate anything on behalf of the Olympia Police Department," Riley authoritatively said.

"It's okay. They're only trying to help. So, I guess I should tell you what I told them?"

"That's a good place to start ma'am," Rands countered. With that Allison recounted how she had used her legs to cutoff the blood flow to the man's brain causing him to pass out after tricking him into taking off her leg restraints before he had a chance to rape her. She didn't get a good look at his face. Nor did she get a chance to look at his house because she was too scared that he would come to and catch her. All that she could remember was the house was dark green and blended in with the trees. She recounted how she just ran and ran and ran until she reached a road that she later learned from the man who picked her up was the old Firmount Highway.

"Thank you so much Mrs. Silson," Riley said.

"Yes, the information you've given us gives us something to start with. Now, we know your kidnapper has a place somewhere out in Hardwick State Forest. That's more than we've had at any time in this case," added

Rands.

Harper Silson busted into the room holding their son. He and Allison embraced each other long and hard with their son sandwiched between the two of them. They remained clutched that way for a long time as Harper and Allison cried with joy on their reunification with dozens of kisses interlaced between the flowing tears. Not wanting to interrupt the happy reunion of the family Riley and Rands quietly exited the room. They were really happy that this family would not have to endure the tragedy of rape that so many others had.

Walking quickly toward the ER's exit, they planned to get out a search party for Hardwick State Forest to hunt down the house. The forest had once been an extremely productive timberland in the early 1900s in the hands of a few different lumber barons. Some of the lumber barons had company towns, mills, and even large private homes for themselves so that they could be close to their operations. Over the decades, many of the buildings had either fallen down or been reclaimed by the forest. Was it possible that the ball-capped rapist had set up shop in one of these derelict houses? Had he altered the house in some way so that it would easily standout? The house probably contained mountains of evidence of past crimes; enough to put him away forever. Hurrying with the hope that they could catch the suspect off guard, Riley and Rands both were on their police-issued cell phones coordinating the efforts to start searching Hardwick State Forest immediately.

Riley and Rands were both extremely tense with emotion and anticipation. Rands face grew red and her armpits sweated profusely as they reached their police car. Her heart raced at the thought of finally being able to slap some cuffs on the piece of shit that had tortured so many women. She was anxious as Riley sped off toward the forest to rendezvous with the other law enforcement officers that they were mobilizing.

Riley was just as agitated. His palms were hot and wet. He was angry at the suspect for what he'd done to these women against their wills. Personally, he wanted the rapist to give him a reason to put a bullet in his head. But the better angels in him convinced him that it would be best if this man went to prison. That he lose his freedom. That he be restrained from any further ability to hurt anyone else. Riley remembered reading literature from neuroscientists explaining how prison for people like the ball-capped rapist is tantamount to torture because they are actively restrained from engaging in the perversions of their choice. Under the influence of reasonable thought once again, Riley turned on the siren to accompany the wildly flashing lights of his vehicle as he entered the freeway.

CHAPTER 30

The ball-capped man quickly loaded items into the back of his large SUV. Without pausing for a moment he placed everything from boxes with coffee mugs and plates to blankets into the back of the SUV with sweat pouring down his face. There was not any method to the madness either. It was if he had received a message that an apocalyptic attack was imminent. Piles of things with no relation to one another were stacked in a precarious manner.

As he loaded the SUV, his mind turned to his earlier narrow escape from what seemed like every law enforcement officer in the world. He knew he might not be so lucky this time. It was all that bitch, Allison's fault this time. He thought maybe he should stay away from women with the letter A in their names. Adrienne nearly got him caught at the Medical Examiner's Office. Now, Allison threatened to do the exact same thing. He promised himself that he would have a day of reckoning with her in the near future. He would teach her a lesson for her disobedience to him. The muscles in his neck were still sore from her strong legs choking him unconscious. But some of the blame belonged to Annie Lone as well. That fucking bitch made him make mistakes in the first place. She personally attacked him in the newspaper. Fuck her. Maybe she needed to learn some respect too.

Turning his focus back to getting the hell out of there before some search party started combing the forest, he realized he had everything of importance out of the place at this point. He walked back inside and slowly took in the aura. The furnishings were those that had occupied his childhood home. He had taken them out of storage after he built this unauthorized forest dwelling using the shell of the old lumber baron's home that once occupied the site. He tried to replicate his childhood home as closely as possible when he constructed the illegal structure. Now he could never return here again.

Slowly doing a walkthrough to make sure nothing with any meaning was left behind, he teared up. Crying, the ball-capped man sadly hung his head. He tried to snap out of it because he knew that it was only a matter of time before police came snooping around. When he finally did get his crying under control about losing his childhood furniture forever, his sadness swiftly turned into anger; unabated rage. He wanted to kill Allison for what she had done to him. She had jeopardized everything by not giving in to him. This was the first time in his life that he felt the desire to kill someone and, strangely, he liked it. He'd always thought himself a peaceful man who never wanted to harm anyone. Fueled by this rage, the ball-capped man went into the basement with a new resolve; the resolve not to leave any evidence for police to find and teach the whore, Allison, a lesson.

Riley parked the unmarked police car he drove in the parking lot at the entrance of one of the walking trails through Hardwick Forest. Soon as he and Rands exited their vehicle he noticed Annie's car parked at the other end of the parking lot.

"Annie's here," Riley said in a worried tone.

"Where is she?" asked Rands.

"I don't know but that's her car," he responded pointing to the other end of the parking lot.

"She sure places herself in some dangerous situations."

"I know. I wish she would listen to me. Come on. Let's see what we can find before the rest of the search party shows up with the K-9s."

No sooner than they started into the narrow path through the dark forest did they both smelled smoke.

"You smell that Riley?" asked Rands.

"Yes. Something's on fire," replied Riley.

Riley also noticed a bright glow coming from a distant area in the forest.

"Looks like whatever is on fire is over there," pointed a slightly agitated Riley with Annie on his mind.

As the two marched off into the dark forest toward the amber glow in the distance, Riley and Rands both worried that Annie had finally met a dreadful end. She had always been so fearless in the face of the danger posed by this ball-capped rapist. Her fearlessness unsettled Rands because she had seen the extent to which some criminals, especially sex offenders, would go to cover their tracks. Nevertheless, Rands respect for the devious and volatile nature of these individuals never waned. She knew that they could snap at any time. Annie seemed to not appreciate that fact, which put her in immense danger.

About a half-hour down the trail, Rands and Riley saw that what was on fire was a structure of some kind about 2,000 yards off the trail. Riley charged headlong off the trail into the dense brush toward the flames. The structure was nearly completely consumed by the flames. Riley looked around the scene frantically. He urgently wanted to make sure that Annie was alright before anything else. Sensing his lack of focus, Rands drew her service weapon and began scanning the location, apprehensive that the person who started the fire might still be nearby.

"Annie! Annie," yelled Riley.

They saw no sign of Annie in the forest. Then amidst the crackling of the fire, Rands heard a rustling sound come from the woods to her right. Peering into the dark forest, she pointed her gun in the direction the sound was coming from.

"Get your hands up!" shouted Rands. "Show me your damned hands."

With that, Riley drew his weapon as well. Two dark shadows emerged from the forest. As they came more into the light of the fire, the detectives saw that the shadows belonged to Annie and Hannah Jane.

"Damn Annie, what the hell are you doing out here?" asked a frustrated Riley re-holstering his weapon.

"Trying to catch up to this asshole who seems to be one step ahead of the police department," responded Hannah Jane.

"Hey! Does your CCO know you're off gallivanting around the woods Hannah Jane? If not, I'm sure I could apprise her of the situation," said a snarky Rands.

"Alright ladies let's all calm down," jumped in Riley. "You two *are* interfering in a police investigation. You shouldn't be out here."

"I know Wilson but we've got to stop this maniac. And besides, he obviously knew you'd be coming out here because he set this place on fire to cover his tracks," Annie explained.

"Of course he did but I don't see why you'd be out here endangering yourself," Riley said with a worried look on his face. He was infatuated by Annie and maybe even loved her but he wasn't about to say it. He just wished she would be more cautious because if the ball-capped rapist thought that she would eventually lead to his arrest he would kill her no sooner than look at her. Knowing this made his stomach feel absolutely sick. Annie poking her nose into this posed a real risk to her safety.

"I've dealt with things far more dangerous than this Wilson. Don't ask me not to help people. Besides, Hannah Jane and I have come up with a plan that will likely lead to the arrest of the rapist. We think that..."

"I know you care about people but people also care about you and you can't go putting yourself in harm's way without considering those people's feelings if something bad happened to you."

Silence fell over them except for the crackling of the fire and the sirens that grew louder in the background. This was the closest that Riley had come to telling Annie he loved her but he hadn't stepped over the line or had he. The silence seemed to be a clear indication that he had said those three damning/flattering words. He told himself that he hadn't said it and that was that. All he'd said was he cared about her.

"Well that was an awkward way to say 'I love you'" joked Hannah Jane trying to ease the tension. "Annie, we'd better get out of here."

"Yea, you're right Hannah Jane. Let's go. We'll talk later Wilson. Okay?"

"Okay Annie."

Annie and Hannah Jane headed back through the brush toward the trail and down the trail back toward the parking lot just as firefighters were reaching the scene of the fire with tools and equipment to attempt to put out the blazing inferno before it spread to the surrounding forest. Annie heard Riley loud and clear but she pushed what he had said out of her mind because she wanted to focus on implementing her and Hannah Jane's plan to capture the rapist. She knew that they probably didn't have a lot of time to implement their plan.

CHAPTER 31

Allison stood in the kitchen by the island tossing a salad smiling while her baby boy played on the floor with a toy truck that he banged against the hardwood. Harper stood outside holding an umbrella in his left hand as he moved around some chicken burgers he had thrown onto the grill. This felt wonderful to Allison. Life with her family. The routine of life. It felt amazing to her.

"Harper, the salad's ready," said Allison before pulling the door to the patio closed. She was a bit annoyed by Harper leaving the door open letting in the cold air. The doorbell rang and Allison looked at the clock on the over-the-range microwave wondering who it could be at this late hour. Allison walked to the front door and peered out the side window next to the door and saw a man dressed in a delivery man's uniform holding a box. She opened the door.

"We're not expecting any packages," Allison said.

"I wasn't expecting you to be such a bitch to me either," said the delivery man.

Allison attempted to close the door but the man at the door muscled his way inside.

"Harper! Harper!" shouted Allison. Harper didn't respond to Allison's cries for help. He couldn't hear her with the door to the patio closed. Eventually, the delivery man pushed the door open and started advancing on her. She kicked him in the crotch but it didn't faze him one single bit.

"I figured you would try that shit again you ungrateful slut. So I came prepared."

"Harper! Help!" she shouted again. He kept coming at her. She backed up and shouted, "Dylan go to your hiding place. Let's play hide and seek."

She knew that this would take him in the opposite direction of the danger in the foyer. Hearing the little boy's feet slap against the hardwood made her feel relieved. With that she began throwing kicks at the ball-capped rapist head and shoulders but he seemed ready for everything she had to dish out because he threw his arms up wildly blocking several of her kicks.

"Get the fuck out of my house you sick son-of-a-bitch."

At that moment, Harper said, "the burgers are ready babe."

"Harper, get a knife!"

"What's going on Allison?" said Harper rounding the corner to see a man in a delivery uniform walking toward his wife. "What the hell are you doing in my house?"

"Shut your fucking mouth you pussy," said the intruder. "I'm here to claim my prize. This bitch wife of yours is going to be mine."

"Fucking asshole," Harper yelled as he ran toward the man and was floored with one blow from the man's fist. He wasn't unconscious but he was seriously dazed. Harper was no fighter. He was no match for the ball-capped rapist.

Allison realized that she had a real problem on her hands now. She was fucking scared and a little bewildered by this fucker appearing out of nowhere but one thing she knew for sure was that she couldn't let him close the distance on her. The number one thing was that she needed to keep her fear in check.

"This is 9-1-1. What's your emergency?"

"My neighbors across the street, the Silsons, their front door is wide open and I think I see someone fighting inside."

"I have dispatched officers to the location. Do you see any weapons?"

"No, I don't."

"When the officers arrive at the scene you should make contact with them."

"Detective Riley," said a uniformed officer passing through the room.

"What up?" replied Riley.

"Isn't that Silson lady the one who escaped from the rape compound the other day?"

"Yes."

"You and your partner better get over to her house. A call just went out over the radio that some kind of incident is happening there right now."

"Shit, I forgot to turn this radio back on," Riley said looking at the radio. Just then Rands stepped out of the restroom.

"What did I miss?" she said when she saw the distressed look on his face.

"Looks like there's some sort of disturbance at Allison Silson's house. We've got to get over there now." The two detectives tore out of the office with an urgency resembling that seen on Black Friday when there are huge sales of big ticket items in some of the retail giants' stores.

Harper was on the ground from the powerful blow delivered by the ball-capped rapist. In that moment, his mind flashed back to the late night call and visit at the front door from Annie and Hannah Jane. Annie begged and pleaded with him to send his wife and kids away because the rapist was possibly coming after Allison again. He didn't heed her warning. He shrugged it off. Why had he done it? Well, for the same dumb reason that most men shrug off warnings. Pride; how could a woman tell him how to protect his family? He knew what needed to be done to keep Allison and Dylan safe. He was, after all, the man of the house. Now, he knew that blowing them off had been a mistake; perhaps a mistake of monumental proportions. He had scoffed when they asked him to let them speak to Allison. Would she understand why he'd done it?

"Alright, bitch. It's just you and me now," said the rapist in an eerie tone.

In a dash, Allison ran into the kitchen. She was followed by the ball-capped rapist. Before he could get to her, she grabbed a large knife from the block and pointed it in his direction.

"You're a feisty little tart," the heavily breathing rapist said. "I think I'm going to enjoy this more than any of the others."

"Get out of my fucking house," Allison screamed.

"You don't mean that baby. We need each other."

"I *need* you to leave me alone."

"Well, that's not going to happen."

A female voice from behind the ball-capped rapist said, "The woman already asked you nicely once to leave. Now, you're just being disrespectful."

He looked over his shoulder and saw Annie Lone. "You're that useless cunt from the women's prison. Aren't you?"

"No, I'm Annie Lone."

"And now that we're done with introductions fuck-face it's time for you to get your sorry excuse for a man ass out of here," Hannah Jane added as she stepped through the door from the dining room. She and Annie both carried large hunting knives.

"I just want you to leave my family alone motherfucker," Allison yelled.

"Don't worry Allison your son is safe across the street with the neighbor," explained Annie.

"We put your husband outside just a few minutes ago and told him to make sure someone has called the police," Hannah Jane joined.

"Thank you guys so much," responded Allison.

The ball-capped rapist reached into the back of his pants and said, "I had hoped it wouldn't come to this but you sluts forced my hand," pulling out a gun. "So drop those knives or I'm going to kill you bitches."

He pointed the pistol around at each of the women wildly because the women occupied his routes of escape. Annie guarded the entry way into the foyer leading out the front door. Hannah Jane stood in the door to the dining room while Allison covered the glass doors leading onto the patio.

"Here's the deal guy. You're going to leave now or…" at that moment the sound of a megaphone pierced the house.

"This is the Olympia Police Department. My name is Sergeant Jed Bailey. I'll be calling the house telephone in ten minutes to talk to you."

He hadn't heard any sirens or anything but it seemed that all possible routes of escape had been cutoff because of these two meddling bitches. He would've had Allison all to himself and been out of the house before any law enforcement showed up. Now it seemed he was trapped. The panic began to set in on him as his mind raced in an effort to plot an exit.

The Olympia SWAT team took up positions all over the neighborhood. The neighbor's house directly across the street had a sniper on the roof to cover the front of the house. Six members of the SWAT team setup in the greenbelt directly behind the Silson home. The negotiator stood discussing with the Incident Commander what the plan of action for dealing with the situation would be.

"What we know at this time is that there is only one man inside the house who poses a threat," said the Incident Commander, Lieutenant Paul Dare. "There are two women in there though who, according to Mr. Silson, saved his son from this monster and are still in there with his wife."

"So we've confirmed he is the so called ball-capped rapist," queried Sergeant Bailey. "Oh yeah, who the hell are the two women in there with Mrs. Silson?"

"Yes we have. Mrs. Silson is the only known victim to escape and she says that this is the guy who kidnapped her. The women are Annie Lone and Hannah Jane."

"So Annie Lone from the Mount Baker women's prison is back at it saving the world. Huh. These civilians ought to leave this stuff to us. Anyway, do we know what's going on in there now?"

"Not yet but the police robot is about to be deployed and will give us a better picture of the goings on with this monster."

A large vehicle labeled <u>SWAT Incident Response Vehicle</u> stopped at the end of the street after maneuvering for a few minutes so that the back of the vehicle faced the officers taking up positions outside the home. In an instant, an officer was setting up a ramp at the open bay of the vehicle to bring the police robot out. Another officer sat with a headset on preparing the robot for deployment into the field. Seeing that all of the cameras on it worked, the SWAT officer operating the robot drove it down the ramp and toward the house to get a look through the window. Jed Bailey, Paul Dare, and others responsible for leadership in this operation saw the police robot and went to join the SWAT officer in the back of the vehicle.

"Alright, you bitches. You should know that I'm a marksman and can probably drop two of you before the third is able to make a move on me with those knives," chided the rapist. "I suggest you put them down and let me out of here."

"That's not going to happen. We can't let you hurt anyone else," Annie replied standing her ground as if anticipating a surprise from the ball-capped lunatic.

"What she's saying is get the fuck out of here," added Hannah Jane. "You're not leaving with anyone but you can go out there and be a man and turn yourself in."

He knew that he was no killer. He'd never killed a person in his life. The earlier desire to kill someone was no longer in him. Perhaps it had only been a passing moment. Yes he'd been extremely angry at other people and he never resorted to that kind of violence but these women were leaving him with few options. Maybe he would have to kill one of them to make his point. Just then he thought of an idea. Without warning, he lunged at Allison holding the gun high and pointed at her face which made her cringe and close her eyes. She closed her eyes long enough for him to knock the knife out of her hands. Annie and Hannah Jane ran to come to her aid but they were too late. He wrapped an arm around her neck and held the gun to her head.

"You two cunts drove me to do this. I'm normally a relatively peaceful guy but you two have gone too far inserting yourself into my business," said the ball-capped rapist as he pressed the cold barrel of the pistol to Allison's temple. The front of his pants felt cold and damp. He looked down at them and saw that they were wet. He realized that Allison had peed. She had also started to cry. He was unshaken by her loss of control.

"Let her go motherfucker," Hannah Jane demanded. She and Annie held their ground. The entire interaction had been captured by the little camera of the police robot peering through the window into the kitchen. Also for the first time ever, the ball-capped rapist didn't have a ball-cap on. It was the first time anyone had seen his face in the midst of his evil actions. He either didn't know that the cap had fallen off when he went after Allison or didn't care. Either way he knew that there was no turning back.

CHAPTER 32

Rands and Riley rushed into the <u>Incident Response Vehicle</u>. Once inside, they both saw the video feed from the police robot. Detective Rands was aghast. She started to shake and tears welled up in her eyes.

"Rands, you okay?" asked a concerned Riley.

"That's Richard," Rands responded with as the blood drained from her face.

"Your Richard? I thought he…oh my God, Irene. I'm so sorry," said Riley placing an arm around her shoulder in an attempt to comfort her.

"What's she saying Riley?" asked Lieutenant Dare.

"That's her boyfriend in there. His name is Richard Lock," replied Riley.

"Her boyfriend's the ball-capped rapist? How could this happen? She didn't know she was shagging a fucking rapist?"

"Alright Lieutenant, back off and focus on the operation. Can't you see she's distraught right now?" said Riley feeling terribly for her and the last thing she needed to hear was some asshole calling her judgment into question.

An officer staring at a computer screen said, "His name is Richard

Adam Lock. Looks like he's an officer at the Department of Fish and Wildlife."

Her face sheet white, Rands' sadness had completely encapsulated her in this moment. She simply stared as tears streamed down both her cheeks. For the first time in a long time she had strong feelings for a man and it turned out he was a serial rapist. A serial rapist who impregnated his victims. A serial rapist who presented as a sweet, loving man when the two of them were together but when he was on his own he wrote declarations of his right as a man to take any woman at any time he wanted. He advocated unwarranted sexual violence against women as if they were nothing more than sexual objects put in place to satisfy his carnal desires. She felt disgusted because she had willingly given herself to him. She hadn't hesitated in lying with him in her bed. Her normally alert creeper radar hadn't given her one warning. Not even in the slightest.

Seeing how pale she had become, Riley guided her to a chair and sat her down.

"Irene, it's okay. Let me get an EMT over here. Here drink this," Riley said handing her a bottle of water taken from a mini-fridge in the back of the <u>Incident Response Vehicle</u>.

Riley felt paralyzed by the situation and he didn't know what to do. He didn't know what to say. She had been alone a long time and finally seemed to have found happiness but now everything was shattered by this son-of-a-bitches treachery. Even more so the rapist threatened the woman he was in love with. Annie was trapped in there with him.

"Alright, I'm going out the front door with Allison. You two are going to get the hell out of my way. I need for her to have my child. She's perfect for it," said the ball-capped rapist slowly dragging Allison toward the foyer.

Just then the telephone began to ring. Annie and Hannah Jane looked at it and then looked at each other.

"I think that's for you," said Hannah Jane jabbing her knife in the direction of the man holding Allison at gunpoint.

"I don't want to talk to them," replied the rapist.

"You have to or they'll come flying in here guns blazing. Then none of us will be walking out of here," said Annie.

"I don't care. I'm not answering it."

"Well, I'll answer it for you," said Annie slowly moving toward the ringing phone in an effort not to provoke the gun wielding idiot. She picked up the receiver and pressed the TALK button and slowly brought the receiver to her ear.

"Hello. Okay. Let me put you on speaker for him," said Annie pressing the SPEAKER button. "The negotiator wants to talk to you Richard. Is that your name Richard Lock?"

"Tell him to fuck off. I'll be leaving with Allison in a minute so I don't need anything," said Richard Lock.

"Richard, this is Sergeant Jed Bailey. I'm with the Olympia Police Department. I just want to talk to you about what's going on in there right now."

"I don't need anything. I don't want…scratch that. I want you guys to pull back off of this block so I can leave. I don't want to hurt Allison but I will if you keep standing in my way."

"Richard, we can't move off of the block. We…"

"Richard how could you?" asked a familiar voice coming from behind over Annie.

Riley looked around and saw that Rands was nowhere to be found. In a panic, he ran outside the Incident Response Vehicle and looked at the car they came in and glanced around the neighborhood but didn't see her. Riley ran back into the Incident Response Vehicle.

"That voice! That's Irene in there," said Riley.

"What's she doing in there?" asked Sergeant Bailey as he hit the mute button on the phone.

"I thought you were watching her," a frustrated Lieutenant Dare yelled as he grabbed a police radio. "Alright team, get ready to go in. We've got a rogue detective inside who may be dangerous. Over."

"Delay that. Over," said Riley over his police radio. "Detective Rands is a professional. You can't go in there guns blazing without knowing if she poses a threat to anyone."

"You've got five minutes and then I'm sending my team in to end this. Got it," Lieutenant Dare said staring at Sergeant Bailey and Riley.

"Bailey, you should try to talk to Irene. Find out what she's up to," said Riley sweating through his shirt.

"Alright, I'll do my best," replied Sergeant Bailey as he took the phone off mute. "Irene, what's going on?" Sergeant Bailey was a seasoned negotiator but this was going to be challenging. He'd never had a fellow officer do what Rands had done. He would have to rely on all of his training at this point to ensure that a nonviolent resolution was reached in this crucial operation.

Emerging from behind Annie Lone pointing her service weapon at Richard's head, Rands had tears streaming down her cheeks. She was devastated to learn that the man she had fallen for was a serial rapist. Rands mind was a jumble. She loved Richard while at the same time she detested his very existence.

"Detective Rands, Sergeant Bailey wants to talk to you," Annie said trying to hand the telephone to her. Rands didn't take the receiver.

"How could you have done this to these women?" Rands asked Richard still pointing her gun at his head.

Richard Lock, still holding Allison with the gun pointed at her head, stared in amazement at the sight of Rands.

"Irene, what are you doing here?" he asked.

"Detective, you should pull back out of the house now," declared Sergeant Bailey. "I won't…"

Before Sergeant Bailey could complete his thought, Rands took the phone from Annie and flung it against the floor shattering it into pieces. Now the <u>Incident Response Vehicle</u> occupants could only see what the police robot could show through the window.

"What are *you* doing here, Richard?" countered Rands.

"I…I."

"Never mind, I don't care," Rands said. "I thought you loved me."

"I do love you, Irene."

"No you don't. You're a sick man, Richard. I can't let you do this to Allison. She's got a family. I've got to stop you."

"Stop me! Why would you want to stop me?"

"You don't have the right to impregnate women against their will."

"It's my God-given right as a man to spread my seed. If I have to make a few women give me what I want then so be it."

"That's exactly why I've got to stop you," a now nearly sobbing Rands said. At that moment, Richard Lock had a strange look come across his face. Annie and Hannah Jane noticed his concern for how Rands saw him differently disappear. He now wore the look of a depraved man.

"Mom, you can't stop me. You couldn't stop me the night I had my way with you and you can't stop me now," Richard exclaimed looking directly into Rands' eyes.

"Mom? Why are you calling me that Richard?" Rands asked.

"I think he just had a break with reality and…" Annie started to say.

"You shut up you slut," Richard shouted pointing the gun at Annie.

"Don't point your gun at me," Annie said. "Rands is not your mother. She's your girlfriend."

"Stop lying to me you fucking cunt. That's my mother right there," yelled Richard pointing his gun in the direction of Rands before putting it back to Allison's head who was now in a hysterical state. "The red hair. The sensual lips. Everything. That's my mother right there. So don't fucking try to lie to me."

"Richard, I'm not your mother," Rands said in an inconsolable condition.

"Mom, why would you lie to me? Remember, the night when I came into your bed. How tender it was? The way things ought to be between mother and son. Being able to put my seed inside you was the best moment of my life."

"Richard, what's wrong with you?" cried Rands.

"It's only natural that a mother and her son come together in that way. I've been so lonely since you left me mommy."

Seeing that Rands was losing control Annie knew that she had to get the gun away from her or she may hurt herself or try to kill Richard and accidentally kill Allison. She had to do something. When Rands wiped tears from her eyes, Annie grabbed hold of the gun and tried to wrest it away from her. Detective Rands regained enough composure to resist. Both women fell to the floor and rolled around fighting for the gun.

"Don't you hurt my mom," yelled Richard trying to draw a bead on Annie with his gun but it was too dangerous to take a shot with both women frantically scrambling for control. Hannah Jane started to come to Annie's aid but he pointed his gun at her and said, "You stay out of it."

While he held off Hannah Jane, Annie used both hands to try to pry the pistol from Rands' fingers. Rands maintained a tight grip on the pistol as Annie tried mightily to get the weapon out of her hand. Rands clawed at Annie's face to no avail. Annie's ferociously went after the gun.

"Stay out of this, Annie," screamed Rands.

With Rands' gun wielding arm held to the floor by Annie placing a knee on it, Rands' fingers went numb and she let the gun go.

Eventually, Annie overpowered the emotionally distraught detective and quickly stumbled to her feet and pointed the gun at Richard Lock. Rands sat up on the floor still crying and panting after the exhausting struggle for the gun.

"Annie, why did you do that?" Rands asked.

"Cause I didn't want you to make a mistake that you'd regret. You have so much to live for Irene."

"You...You're right," Rands whispered. She sat on the floor and thought for a moment. Then she got to her feet and looked at Richard Lock. "Come on son, let's get out of here."

Annie and Hannah Jane stood watching with dumbfounded looks on their faces. They were in complete disbelief.

"Get out of here? Where will we go? How will we get pass the police outside?" asked Richard.

"Don't worry about that. They'll let us out. I'm a detective. They won't stop me."

After considering what she'd said, Richard slowly loosened his grip on Allison's neck until she was free except for his hand remaining resting on her shoulder. She eventually collapsed to the floor relieved that the ball-capped rapist was finally, it appeared, turning his attention away from her.

"Okay, mom," Richard said. "But first I need to plant my seed in Allison."

"No! We've got to go," said Rands.

"I can't. I must give her my baby," he exclaimed.

Richard started tugging at his belt buckle with his left hand. He placed the gun he held on the kitchen counter freeing his right hand so that he could completely take off his pants.

"You should give me the baby, son," Rands said. "Not her. She's not worthy of carrying your baby."

"But I want Allison too!"

"She already has a husband, Richard."

"I don't care. She's going to be mine."

At this point, Richard was standing in the room only wearing his boxers. He picked up his gun and pointed it at Allison.

"Stand up Allison," Richard barked.

"What?" said Allison.

"You heard me. Get the fuck up," Richard shouted while pulling her to her feet with his left hand. He pressed the gun to Allison's head. "Pull your fucking pants down and bend over."

Allison slowly pulled down her pants and began crying again.

"When I'm finished, mom, then we'll go," Richard said looking in the direction of Rands.

As Richard forcefully bent Allison over, he pulled out his erection and prepared to put it inside the now exposed Allison. Three loud pops went off in the room. In a flash, Richard fell against Allison's back before sliding hard to the floor. Annie stood holding a .38 revolver still pointing in the direction of the now mortally wounded Richard.

At the sound of the three gunshots, the SWAT team and every other officer charged into the house with their firearms drawn and at the ready. Once inside, they saw Richard's body lying on the floor and bleeding heavily. Upon entering, Riley found his partner, Rands, crying hysterically and staring at Richard's dying body. He went to her side to console her.

He felt a twinge of pain in his heart. This was the first time his partner and dear friend had found love. He simply placed an arm around her in an effort to comfort his closest friend.

In the aftermath, it was learned that Annie shot Richard to stop him from raping Allison in front of them. Allison, Hannah Jane, Rands, and Annie all stated that Rands had a .38 revolver in an ankle holster and pulled the gun when Richard was about to rape Allison but didn't pull the trigger. To save Allison from suffering this violent attack by Richard, Annie snatched the gun from Rands and pulled the trigger three times. So with it well documented that Annie had used deadly force to prevent serious bodily injury to another person, the police didn't take her into custody. Rands on the other hand was still nearly inconsolable even an hour and a half after the shooting.

Rand's tears continued uninterrupted while staring at the body bag containing Richard's body. She understood that Richard had to be stopped but she couldn't do it. She couldn't shoot him. She loved him too much. He had been so gentle to her. He had made her happy. Even though he was about to rape someone, Rands couldn't kill the man she had fallen in love with. EMTs spoke to Rands who was despondent and unresponsive to their questioning. Riley asked them to take her to the hospital for an emergency mental health evaluation. He let her know that he would be there as soon as possible to check on her as an EMT closed the ambulance doors. As he turned to walk away, he saw Annie and Hannah Jane and walked toward them.

"Annie, you okay?" Riley asked.

"Yes. Yes, I am," she replied.

"Can we have a moment, Hannah Jane?" asked Riley.

"Yeah, Yeah I know. You two love birds want some privacy," Hannah Jane said before stalking off in the direction of the car they had arrived in.

"Annie I was so scared that something was going to happen to you in there."

"Nothing…" but before she could finish Riley pulled her into an embrace holding her close to him. She responded by wrapping her arms around him. A warm feeling came over her in that instant. She now knew that he cared about her simply from the strength and emotion of his embrace. When they finally let each other go, they both felt a little awkward because of the way they allowed themselves to just let go in such a public place.

"Annie, never do anything like that again. My heart can't take it."

"Sorry but I had to help you all pin this guy down and I figured that the odds were that he was going to go after the one that got away. He had gone so far that he probably felt endangered after she got a good look at his face."

"Well, you should retire from your unofficial position as *law keeper*. I'm glad you have such a big heart and want to make society a better place but if you meet a nice guy who is interested in seriously dating you and maybe even marrying you, I'm sure he wouldn't be happy with you putting yourself at risk like that."

"What do you mean 'if I meet a nice guy'?"

"I didn't mean it that way."

"Oh, I'm just kidding. But you should know that I think that I already have," and with that Annie grabbed Riley's face, pulled him to her, and placed a big lingering kiss on Riley's lips.

"Wow, Annie! Thanks."

"Now get over to the hospital and check on your partner. When you get some free time call me."

"Definitely will," said Riley with a huge smile on his face.

Annie watched as Riley hurried toward his cruiser before heading toward her own car with Hannah Jane looking out the back window in her direction.

"You two really are going to have to bump some uglies eventually to relieve some of that tension. That big, handsome man is just what the doctor ordered for you girl," smiled Hannah Jane.

"You make it sound so romantic Hannah Jane."

"I do my best," laughed Hannah Jane.

"But on the serious side Hannah Jane, thank you for being there for me. I really appreciate you friendship and bravery. You followed me into one of the most dangerous situations. I don't know how to express my gratitude to you."

"Stop being ridiculous. You don't owe me any gratitude or anything else. Your friendship and helping me see that there is a better way to live my life is enough. I love you Annie and I would walk through hell with gasoline drawers on for you."

"I love you too Hannah Jane."

Both women felt a great deal of relief that the outcome hadn't resulted in the other person's serious injury or death at the hands of the rapist. They knew that things could've gone very badly that evening but fortune was on their side. Now, they could focus on living their lives together. After all, they were best friends. Who needed anything more.

CHAPTER 33

Hannah Jane walked through the front door of the house to find Riley embracing Annie who was sitting on the couch talking to Sibyl.

"What the hell are you guys up so late for?" asked Hannah Jane.

"Waiting for you to get home," Sibyl chimed in.

"Yeah, we just wanted to know how your date went," yawned Riley.

"How in the hell did you guys know that I would be coming in," said Hannah Jane lying her keys and purse on the kitchen counter.

"Cause you told us that you were going to try a different approach with this guy," Annie said.

"Oh you mean, I said I wouldn't spread my legs right away?"

"Um, yes," replied Sibyl.

"Well, I still could have stayed at his place and cuddled naked with him," said Hannah Jane.

"Well, I think that cuddling naked with a guy usually leads to something happening," Annie.

"I was just joking," Hannah Jane said as she sat down on the couch next to Sibyl.

"So how was the date?" asked Sibyl.

"Gerald was a perfect gentleman. All that shit had me so turned on. I really like him. I wish I could throw his ass down and take advantage of him but I took your advice and decided to try it your way. You know, get to know him better and all first. But now I have to get myself off tonight. Thanks a lot by the way," Hannah Jane said looking at Sibyl and Annie with an annoyed look on her face.

"I hope everything works out for you guys," Annie said looking at her watch. "Well, I think Wilson and I are going to turn in for the night."

Riley and Annie both got up and stretched and yawned.

"So you two just gon' leave and go screw your brains out while a girl is here struggling," smiled Hannah Jane.

"Hannah Jane! We're just going to sleep," a reddening Annie said.

"Well, goodnight you two," said Hannah Jane.

"Goodnight," said Sibyl.

"Goodnight ladies," yawned Riley.

Riley and Annie both lay in the middle of the bed embracing each other buried in Annie's big fluffy down comforter. Annie loved being held by Riley. He was exactly what she wanted. A man who was gentle and caring. It had been a long time since she felt that and it was good. She didn't have any idea where this relationship was going but at the moment it didn't matter.

"Annie, I hope you have officially retired from crime fighting? It makes me worry way too much. I don't know what I would do if something happened to you," Riley said caressing Annie's shoulder.

"I can't guarantee that I'll ever stop trying to help women who are being abused or attacked. But I will try to do whatever it is I decide to do in the safest way possible," smiled Annie before planting a kiss on Riley's lips.

She slowly climbed on top of Riley until she straddled him and stared into his eyes.

"What are you doing?" asked Riley.

"What do you think I'm doing?" Annie responded.

"I love you, Annie," Riley whispered.

"I love you too," said Annie before passionately kissing Riley.

The two lovers allowed their desire for one another to control them as they kissed and caressed each other. Riley was head over heels for Annie and never thought that he would be this crazy in love with someone. He wanted to spend every waking moment with Annie. He wanted to hold her, be near her, and generally be involved in every part of her life. Now, that he had her he was going to be everything thing that she ever wanted.

The next day a smiling Annie sat across from CCO Vonde. It was her last day of her conditional pardon. Her pardon was now going to become fully effective. She would no longer be a convicted felon. She would have full freedom to travel anywhere at any time without having to report to anyone. CCO Vonde stood up from behind her desk grinning with her hand out to shake Annie's but she wound up being pulled into a hug by Annie.

"Thank you CCO Vonde for everything," Annie said still holding the hug.

"Call me McKenzie and you did it all yourself," replied CCO Vonde as they released the hug. "What's next for you lady?"

"I'm just going to enjoy my life CC…McKenzie. Enjoy my life with my mom, Julia, Hannah Jane, Sibyl, and Wilson. Other than that, I don't have any other plans. I have everything I need."

"That's wonderful Annie. That's truly what life is all about. Enjoying the time you have with those that you love. Take care of yourself."

"What about you McKenzie?"

"I'm going to keep trying to help as many offenders coming out of prison and jail as I can. I've got to keep on going."

With that both women said their final goodbyes and parted ways. CCO Vonde opened the file folder on her desk and got back to work. Annie walked out of the office for the last time ready to take on the challenges of life.

ABOUT THE AUTHOR

Charles Malone is also the author of *The Rise of Annie Lone*. He lives in the Pacific Northwest with his wife and children. Follow him on Twitter @CharlesLMalone and Facebook for updates on his upcoming projects and other news.

www.ingramcontent.com/pod-product-compliance
Lightning Source LLC
Chambersburg PA
CBHW030253130626
46549CB00002B/506